CHEATING
DEATH

By the same author

CHEATING DEATH

H.R.F. KEATING

THE MYSTERIOUS PRESS

Published by Warner Books

A Time Warner Company

® Mysterious Press books are published by Warner Books, Inc.,
1271 Avenue of the Americas, New York, NY 10020.

 A Time Warner Company

The Mysterious Press name and logo are registered trademarks of Warner Books, Inc.

Printed in the United States of America
First published in Great Britain 1992 by Hutchinson
First U.S. printing: September 1994

10 9 8 7 6 5 4 3 2 1

Library of Congress Cataloging-in-Publication Data

Keating, H. R. F. (Henry Reymond Fitzwalter), 1926-
    Cheating death / H.R.F. Keating.
      p. cm.
    ISBN 0-89296-512-6
    1. College students—India—Fiction. 2. Cheating (Education)-
-Fiction. I. Title.
PR6061.E26C48 1992
823'.914—dc20
                                        94-9502
                                          CIP

1

There was nothing else for it. He would have to beat his wife.

Inspector Ghote sat at his desk, paperwork forgotten, and for the twentieth, thirtieth, fortieth time began to go over in his mind everything that had brought him to this point of decision.

But wait, he said to himself almost as soon as he had begun. Wait. Was he really going to do that? Other husbands did, of course. Other Crime Branch officers even. And cheerfully boasted about it, gup-shupping in quiet moments of the day. Only way to keep the biwi in her place, they said. One good beating every now and again, and no nonsense after about who is making the decisions. Only way to do it. But . . . But was he really going to do that himself? Take one of the chappals off his feet or find something else and beat Protima? Yet he had good reason. Definitely.

There was what she had done about Ved going to college, if nothing else. He felt a happy blossoming of revived rage at the thought of that. When it was obvious, with the boy's interest in science and computers and all, that he should go to somewhere like Bombay's famed St Xavier's Technical Institute, what had Protima done? Sitting at the annual police awards ceremony, by chance next to the wife of the Dean at Elphinston College, she had contrived, whispering away while the medals on their velvet cushions were being taken up to be pinned to deserving chests, to arrange that Ved should be admitted when the time came in first year at Elphinston. That venerable academic institution, not at all suitable for the boy, just because she and he had been students there together long ago when he had first come to Bombay.

And, after all, that had been just only the last straw on to the camel's back. Nowadays it was she who was making each and every decision in their lives. It was high time he stopped just sitting there, grin and bear.

He looked at his watch. Near enough to end of office hours.

Yes, he could leave now, go straight home and do it. It would be a first-class time as a matter of fact. Ved was due to be at a meeting of the Regals

Cricket Club – he was in line to be elected captain – so there would be no problem about him being about the place when it was happening.

Yes.

He pushed back his chair, got to his feet, shoved his papers into a drawer. And his phone rang.

He stood where he was, looking at it. Answer or not answer? If he had made up his mind to go just two minutes earlier, he would not have been in the cabin to hear. But what if it was the Additional Commissioner? It was never very much of a good idea to let your boss find you out of your seat even a few minutes early.

He picked the phone up. It was the Additional Commissioner.

Ghote's first thought as he had climbed the circular stair up to the balcony outside the head of Crime Branch's office was that he might not now, if he was to be given some task, be able to go through with the beating business. He had felt then a twinge of relief which had surprised him. Yet, after all, he had said to himself, the point was his decision had been taken. One hundred percent. So natural enough, isn't it, to be somewhat pleased not have to do anything about it for the time being?

But, standing at attention now in front of the Additional Commissioner's wide sweep of a desk, he could not help asking himself why he was being told he had to go ek dum to this Oceanic College, miles away it seemed up beyond Malad Creek at the outer edge of sprawling Bombay. By the time he had reached the place at this late hour of the day it was very doubtful if anyone in authority would still be there. And the sort of inquiries he was expected to make, if he had understood correctly, could be carried out only with tact and discretion. Certainly not rushed into.

'But, sir,' he ventured. 'Tomorrow itself I would – '

'Inspector, I do not think you have at all grasped what it is at stake. This is a matter involving the Centre, Ghote. The Centre. You know what has been happening in Bombay University. Scandal after scandal. State Ministers involved. Those fellows getting nephews and daughters and what-all into colleges when they are not at all possessing requisite number of marks, and then next month, say, college in question being granted right to take extra students thereby gaining very much of capitation monies from State funds. Partymen getting a damn bad reputation. Naturally Delhi is interested.'

'Yes, sir,' Ghote thought he ought respectfully to put in.

The Additional Commissioner shot him a look as much as to accuse him of doubting the importance of what he had been told.

'Oh, I know, Inspector, things in Bombay are not as bad as in other places. In Delhi itself last year 3,400 cheats in exams were reported. In Kanpur, I think it was, they had three rooms for their BSc exam, one at Rupees 1,000 where you could cheat on your own, one at Rupees 2,000 where you could take the help of the invigilators themselves and a Rupees 5,000 room where you could call for answers from outside. With that sort of thing alleged to be going on, no wonder Government is alerted to each and every new case.'

'Yes, sir, yes.' Ghote infused eagerness into his voice.

But evidently still not enough.

'Read this damn report then,' the Additional Commissioner stormed. 'Read the report those CBI fellows who were air-dashing here have left. Read it. Read it.'

He darted furious glances here, there and everywhere over the broad surface of his big semi-circular desk, plucked up the heavy little silvery discs of his paperweights left and right and eventually located the report. He thrust it at Ghote.

Taking it, Ghote's immediate reaction was how slight it was. A single sheet and no more. Surely if this business was so important that officers from the Central Bureau of Investigation had been sent hurrying down by air to Bombay, the report they had made ought to be bulkier than this. And why, in any case, had they gone back to Delhi with their investigation not completed?

Standing, still at attention, in front of the wide desk, on which the Additional Commissioner's peon, who had crept into the big room, was at that moment neatly laying down a single little round black mat preparatory to placing on it a cup of tea, he read.

Investigation into Theft and Subsequent Sale of Papers in Statistical Techniques in University of Bombay BCom Examination.
Upon arrival in Bombay at 1400 hours, June 7, we proceeded to question one Subhash Sarkar, final year BCom student at Elphinston College, Bombay, previously arrested by officers from Azad Maidan PS as being in possession of a question paper for an exam not then due to be held. We were able rapidly to ascertain that the said paper had been obtained, for the sum of Rupees 50 from one Bala Chambhar, student at Oceanic College, residing at Chawl No 4, Dadasaheb Phalke Marg, opp. Vishnu Shoe

Clinic, Dadar, Bombay 400014. Pursuing investigation at Oceanic College, we further ascertained that the said stolen paper was obtained from the locked chamber of the Principal, Dr Shambu S. Bembalkar, on Monday, June 5, at some time between 1300 hours and 1330 hours, Principal Bembalkar being the sole holder of the key to the said chamber. We were, however, unable to ascertain by what method the said Bala Chambhar had obtained entry since, proceeding to locate and arrest the said culprit, investigations revealed he had been taken to KEM Hospital. At the aforementioned hospital we ascertained that the said Bala Chambhar, patient under care of Dr P. P. Shah, was in a state of coma, believed due to attempted suicide by poison. This state of coma is liable to persist until the expiry of said patient and we were therefore unable to pursue further inquiries. Signed—

'Well, man. Don't take all day. Simple enough. Fine example of concise and accurate report. First-class fellows those CBI wallas. Now, are you fully understanding what is your duty in the matter?'

Ghote would have liked to have answered 'No'.

'Yes, sir, yes,' he said, however. 'The CBI inquiry must have been altogether bogged down owing to the culprit being in state of coma. And, as you were saying, sir, it is nevertheless one hundred percent vital to find out exactly how the paper, the said paper, was stolen from that locked chamber. And I am to do that, sir, so that a full report to the Centre may be made.'

Yet even as the words poured out he could not prevent himself wondering just how hundred percent vital it all was. The CBI men had traced the leak after all, though that had been something not in fact too difficult. So what was all the urgency to be able to say exactly how the paper had been removed from a chamber that was said to be locked?

Well, anything from the Centre . . .

'And, Ghote, I want that report not next year, or next month, or next week. I want it just as quickly as those CBI chaps were putting in theirs. Understood?'

'Yes, sir.'

'Which is why, Ghote, you will proceed to this place, Oceanic College, whatever that is, now. Now.'

'Yes, sir.'

'Well, look for it on my map, Inspector, and get to hell out there.'

With an imperious finger the Additional Commissioner pointed to the huge map of Greater Bombay and its police districts that hung on his wall.

Ghote hurried over, sweat springing up all over his back despite the two big ceiling fans that fluttered the documents under the paperweights on the desk and brought a little welcome coolness to the humid June heat. To his relief, he spotted at once the words 'Oceanic College', inked in approximately where he had first looked. The place was, he saw, even further from Crawford Market headquarters than he had thought. He would have a weary and miserable trip out there, almost certainly find no one to talk to, nothing happening, and then have to endure a long and miserable trip back home.

By which time, he realised, it would be much, much too late to do what he had finally decided on just before the Additional Commissioner had called him. So that matter would have to be postponed till . . .

But another thought struck him.

If he was going to have to go all the way out to this Oceanic College this evening, then it was perfectly reasonable to interpret the Additional Commissioner's 'now' with a certain amount of latitude. It would be asking too much, for example, for him to go all that distance and begin inquiries straightaway without taking some time for food. And food was best taken at home. Protima would have prepared a meal in fact. But, if he were to set off for home this minute, he would arrive well before the Regals meeting had reached the point of electing the team captain. So there would be nothing to prevent him doing the needful with Protima. Today. This evening. Almost at once.

He gulped.

2

In the road outside his home Ghote paused and took stock.

Yes, there was no doubt about it. What he had decided on must be done. Things had gone too far. There was one only way to put a halt to it. Just what they all said, mulling over life in general in the canteen or out taking a cold drink somewhere. Every now and again a woman, unless you are lucky enough to have found a real example of a good Hindu wife, needs a good thrashing up.

And, certainly, Protima had got to the point of having to be put in her place. That business of going behind his back and seeking a favour through the wife of the Dean at Elphinston, it had been the end only of a long, long line creeping up from the smallest beginnings.

Yes, how different it all was now from the first days of their marriage, even though he had known then that Protima was someone with opinions of her own. That he had realised the very first time he had set eyes on her. He could see her now, standing up in the lecture room and actually challenging what the lecturer had said. The only girl with the guts to do it. What a moment that had been.

And then, later, she had, wonderfully, shown an equal independence. At a time when arranged marriages were even more the accepted way than nowadays, to have insisted on making a love match.

A sudden flash of memory showed him lying with his head on her thigh when at last with difficulty they had found a patch of ground somewhere unfrequented – where had that been? – and she had let the pallu of her sari fall down from her head as she had leant over him to shroud him in her dark descending hair and over that the cotton's bluey green shade.

Oh, and in their first married years she had been a model Hindu wife, wholly devoted to her husband, dutiful, obedient, taking care always to serve him his favourite dish. The sweet carrot halwa he had once told her his mother used to make so well. Of course, it had been a sort of play-acting. They had both known it. Yet she had truly given him the place of honour in those days. Definitely.

Now though. Now the see-saw had swung one hundred percent the other way. She was up and he was down. Now she was the one, it seemed, who said always what was to be done. He was the one who, sooner or later, did it. High time to put an end to that.

It must really have begun, he thought, with the arrival of little Ved, now by no means so little. It had been natural enough then that she, the woman, the mother, should know what ought to be done for, first, the baby and as time went on for the growing child. And he himself had been altogether willing to follow. But that situation had gone on. And on. Grown and grown.

Until this last unforgivable thing.

He marched forward. On reaching his door he administered the sharpest of raps on its outer latch.

The door opened.

'What for are you home so early?' Protima demanded.

He found himself speechless. Somehow he could not reply to that abrupt question by saying with blank brutality, 'I have come to give you one good beating'. But he was at once determined that he would not answer with a meek explanation of his having to go out on duty and wanting to take food before he set off.

'It is not so early,' he got out at last.

'But are you expecting food to be ready?' Protima banged back. 'How can I be knowing just only when you are wanting?'

He decided that this, vigorously though it had been put, acknowledged enough that it was a wife's duty to provide food just as soon as the husband required it. So he could say now that he did in fact need something to eat as soon as it could be got.

And Protima went at once into the kitchen. Even though as she turned away every line in her body expressed sharp disapproval of a husband who could make such a demand.

It was a disapproval reinforced by the length of time she chose to take in getting something cooked. He knew well enough that the preparations necessary for what she had intended to provide that evening – it was seldom nowadays that she asked him in the morning if there was anything he would particularly like – would have been made well in advance. So, in fact, it should not have taken more than a few minutes to give the food its finishing touches on the stove. But time went by and went by and no appetising odour emerged from the little room at the back.

Should he call out and ask how long she would be? But he had failed to say in the first place that he was under orders to go out to Oceanic College with all speed. If he was to say this now, she would take it into her head that he had invented the need for haste by way of a rebuke.

So he sat where he was. And fumed.

Should he forget about having something to eat? Storm into the kitchen at this moment, seize Protima by the arm, drag her out here and do what had to be done?

But what exactly had to be done? It was all very well for his canteen cronies to boast about 'giving the biwi a good thrashing up', but they never mentioned the details. What did they do it with? What would be fair-play only? How did they ensure that, far from being just only the awarding of due and proper punishment, the business did not end up as one undignified struggle?

No, this was not the time. The whole thing needed to be thought out with very much more of care.

But, after only a little longer, he was unable to prevent himself creeping over to the kitchen doorway and parting the bead curtain an inch or two.

But it was two inches too much.

'I am getting as quickly as I can,' Protima turned and said. 'Why must you be so impatient?'

He returned to his chair.

More minutes passed. He began to suspect that, had he not gone to the kitchen, he would not still be waiting. But there did not seem to be anything he could do about that now. At least some spicy odours were beginning to float in. Twistingly hungry though they were making him.

At last Protima came in with the thali. The little heaps of food on it looked every bit as delicious as their wafting smells had indicated. But he felt he had to wolf them down fast as he could.

All very well to have thought as he was leaving Headquarters that it would be one hundred percent fair to stop at home for some quick sustenance. But he had been here already far longer than he had counted on.

'I am not knowing why I take trouble to cook when you are eating like a pi-dog only,' Protima said.

'Hurry. Must go.'

He rose from the table, mouth still full and with a vague gesture that could have meant anything – 'Thank you for getting food so quickly' or 'Wait, and you will find out who is giving orders here' – he left almost at a run.

But it was well past dark before at last he located Oceanic College. At first, from the unlit, deserted road on which it lay all he could make out in the light of a solitary bent street-lamp, was a wide stretch of grass with beyond it the faint outlines of what looked like a building constructed not many years before, all slabby concrete and sharp rectangles, even after he had gone right up to the padlocked gate in the high surrounding railing. Every window was blank and lightless. The sole massive door he could just make out as a darker patch on the white front wall was firmly shut. There was no sign even of a watchman.

Very well, he said to himself, I will be able to report tomorrow that as per instructions I came here and the only one fact I was able to discover is that Oceanic College is altogether damn far from any part of the sea.

Only, much as I would be liking to say same to Additional Commissioner sahib, he added, I know to one hundred percent I will not at all risk uttering same.

He gave a weary shrug and began to turn away.

But then there just caught his eye at a corner of the big building a glimmer of light. It was not from any electric bulb or neon tube, or even from a flashlight. It might have been the light of a match, only it looked larger and stronger.

He stepped closer to the tall surrounding railing and peered between two of the bars, their iron cool on his forehead.

At once he saw a second distant point of light split off from that first, and then a third and a fourth. Then he realised what it was he was watching. Torches, tar-soaked sticks, being lit one from another. And, as quickly, he guessed what they were being lit for. It would be for a night morcha.

Yes, some people were taking out a procession of protest. Students, no doubt. Only young hotheads would think that any protest would be more effective for being carried out by torchlight. And only dreamy students would be so idiotic as to protest where nobody would see.

And what would they be protesting about? Was this in any way connected with the business he had been sent out here for? Were perhaps Bala Chambhar's fellow students objecting to police inquiries? Inquiries which, it seemed, had driven the boy to attempt suicide? Had put him into the coma that had blocked further investigations?

A sudden spurt of determination fountained up in his mind. Yes, by God, he would show those chaps. If they had gone flying back to Delhi, leaving that unfledged chick of a report behind them, well, he would find the answer to how the Statistical Techniques question-paper had been taken from that locked chamber and show them just what a simple Bombay detective could do. By God, he would.

And – the thought suddenly struck him – could it be that those students down by the college building might at least give him some line to go on in the morning when he came back here and questioned the Principal and any other staff members who ought to know what might have happened? If his own distant college experience was anything to go by, students delighted in gossips and rumours about their lecturers, the more senior the better. And about their fellow students too. So he might well learn something here. He very well might.

In the distance the torches now had grown to be twenty or more in number and were burning well. By their brighter light he could make out a huddle of figures and, above them, a dozen or more placards, showing palely white in the humidly thick surrounding darkness.

They were too far away for him to be able to read the slogans that would be scrawled on them. But it would not be long before the march began and then he would perhaps get an idea of what Bala Chambhar's fellow students thought about the theft of the question-paper.

Quietly he slipped away along beside the college's high railing until he came to a patch of dense shadow underneath a thick-leaved neem tree. There he waited.

In less than two minutes the head of the procession of protest had reached the gate. Evidently someone had possessed themselves of a key to its padlock, easy enough to 'borrow', because after a short pause and a good deal of wavering from the leading torch the wide gates were drawn back, the harsh squeal of metal on concrete plain to be heard over the distant excited chattering.

Then he saw the morcha set off in earnest. Torches held more steadily. Placards lifted in defiance. And a steady chanting beginning to rise up.

'Autocracy murdabad!'

'Principal Bembalkar out! Out, out, out!'

'Autocracy murdabad!'

'Princi, resign! Resign! Resign!'

So they were demanding that Dr Shambu Bembalkar should quit his post. Why? Could it be because he had somehow let that question-paper be stolen from his chamber? Had done something wrong? Or failed to do something he should have?

The shouts, often jumbled one on top of the other, were continuing. He listened hard in the darkness and soon made others out.

'We demand right to write BCom!'

'Autocracy murdabad!'

'Give us back our exam!'

'Autocracy murdabad! Princi resign!'

Ah, so that was it. They had been ready to write their Bachelor of Commerce exam, and because of the theft it had been cancelled. So they were protesting, making their feelings felt. Under the safe cover of darkness.

Well, all right. Young men must let off steam somehow.

Now, as the head of the procession got nearer his neem-tree lurking place, he was able even by the chancy light of the torches to read what was written on the upraised placards, much though they were bobbing up and down in time to the chanting.

Exam Cancel Unfair – We Demand Right to Cheat – You Rig Elections Let Us Rig Exams – Bring Back BCom Exam Now

He blinked.

Were these full-scale idiots really and truly insisting that an exam for which one paper at least had been leaked up and down entire Bombay should all the same be held? What sort of a madhouse was it where he was going to have to make his inquiries?

3

Ghote was so astonished that he almost let the morcha go out of sight into the thick darkness between the rare light-poles along the road. Then he remembered with a jerk that it had been his intention to find out as much as he could about Oceanic College from the protesters. He might, if he was very lucky, actually get to know a possible way in which the Statistical Techniques question-paper had been removed from the Principal's locked chamber.

He shot out of his place of concealment under the neem-tree and set off at a loping run after the straggling, chanting line of placard carriers. Soon enough he caught up with the rear rank. But, reckoning that anyone timid enough to choose that safe position in a demonstration would not be much use to him, he ran on a few steps more and fell into step beside another small cluster of protesters. Only to find himself walking shoulder to shoulder with a girl.

'Miss, Miss,' he blurted out, all other considerations chased from his head by the discovery of the daughter of some respectable, educated family out alone in the hours of darkness with a mob of hothead boys. 'Miss, what is it you are doing here at nine – ten o'clock in the night? Are your parents knowing? What do you mean by it all?'

In the sideways glance he had given the girl he had seen she was appallingly young, perhaps only just seventeen, dangerously young. And, so far as he could see, she was pretty too, dangerously pretty. Her light-green patterned sari shimmered and swayed in the torchlight as she strode purposefully along, proudly holding up one of the placards. If only she knew as much as any police officer about what might happen to a young, pretty girl out late in the night . . .

His outburst had caused her to come to a full check in the middle of a particularly loud 'Princi out, out, out'. But now she broke into a peal of laughter. Lively laughter and free.

'Miss,' he said sharply once more.

'Oh, grandpapa,' the girl spluttered out. 'You should be the one going home. Home to where you can be shutting your eyes to what the world is now like.'

Grandpapa. Indignation bloomed in Ghote's head. The impudent little wretch. Why, what she needed was a good hiding.

And, as that notion flickered across his mind, he saw suddenly that this laughing, marching, demonstrating little creature was, change for change, just what his Protima had been all those years ago when they had been at Elphinston College together.

The thought robbed him for some time of speech.

'Autocracy murdabad,' the shout rose in front and behind into the unresponsive dark. 'Princi resign, resign, resign.'

'Well, well,' he brought himself to say at last, stepping out still beside this shimmering green young thing, 'Perhaps you are not wrong to one hundred percent. I was, perhaps, speaking somewhat as a grandpapa. And, I am assuring, I am not so old as that.'

Again the girl spluttered with half-concealed laughter.

'Then, Mister Not-so-old,' she said, 'what is it you are doing talking to a young girl you are meeting in the night only?'

A new wave of indignation rose up in him.

'What I am – What I am doing?'

He took in a breath.

'Very well,' he said, coming to a decision. 'I will be telling you what it is I am doing. I am a police officer. Crime Branch. Inspector Ghote by name. And I have come out here to Oceanic College because it was from the chamber of your Principal that a certain exam question-paper has been stolen.'

'And that is such a great crime that you come, ek dum, hurrying out here at – what were you saying? – ten o'clock in the night?' the girl retorted. 'Inspector sahib, you should be investigating into worse matters than this. There are many, many in this city robbing the poors by selling adulterated foods. There is slumlordism, altogether unchecked. There are people taking the fattest of bribes. Why, if you are able to deal just only with small affairs, there are plenty – plenty eve-teasers for you to be putting behind the bars.'

She turned away to toss a quick 'Autocracy murdabad' up to the starlit sky.

'When I am ordered to arrest some boy for molesting a girl,' Ghote said, holding in with an effort a new spurt of fury, 'I will do same. But for now I am dealing with the cognisable offence of theft, and I am thinking that you may be able to assist.'

Then, before the scorn he had seen rising up could break out in words, he leapt in again.

'To assist as is your citizen's duty.'

And it seemed that his appeal to the young person's sense of justice, something he had clearly detected in the girl's talk of the robbers of the down-trodden, had struck home.

For the length of time that it took her to stride out another dozen paces she was silent, not rising even to a modest echo of a spate of 'Princi resign' coming from in front. Then she answered, and in an altogether less assured way.

'Well, it is not right, I suppose, to steal even exam papers. But, Inspector, you should know that when so many people with influence and connections are getting the bad marks of their kins and kith here in college graced, as they say, then all must be fair in love and war.'

Ghote pounced on the note of failing assurance in her claim.

'Now, Miss, you are knowing better than that. Stealing is stealing. You know it.'

'Well, all right. Bala should not have taken that paper. It is just only what you would expect from him, as a matter of fact.'

'Ah, yes? This Bala – Bala Chambhar, isn't it? – he is some sort of a notorious badmash?'

But this seemed too much for the girl.

'You police,' she shot out. 'Always thinking because someone is one of the poors they cannot be doing good.'

Her voice lifted in a defiant 'Autocracy murdabad'.

'But,' Ghote replied steadily, 'this fellow Bala – he is not a well-off fellow, yes? – was he always doing good only?'

For another pace or two the girl did not reply. Once she essayed a muted 'Princi resign' but her fellow protesters had tired for the moment of shouting to utterly empty surroundings and her voice was the only one to be heard. Then she turned to him once more.

'No, you are right. Although Bala is here at college on the minority rights list as a harijan, he is, true, almost all the time a liar, cheat and thief, a bully also.'

'So Bala would know each and every trick of HB?' he ventured.

'HB? What it is?'

Oh, young, young, young, Ghote thought. Too young and innocent even to know that HB is house-breaking.

He explained.

'Oh, yes, yes. I knew really, only . . . But, Inspector, I cannot help you actually. I mean, I know Bala was, yes, a badmash. Everyone is knowing that. But what exactly he was doing he kept always to himself.'

'No boasting?' Ghote asked. 'No telling how he knew a way of getting into one locked room? No wanting to be showing off to a pretty girl like yourself only?'

But for that he got a renewed sharp look.

'No, Mr Policeman. No.'

Well, he thought in the deepest privacy of his head, when I was succeeding all those years ago at last to tell Protima she was pretty she was not at all objecting.

For a vivid instant he saw her then as she had been in those distant days, at the very moment he had managed to bring out his compliment – he heard his own ridiculously strangled voice too – and saw the way she had quickly brought up the pallu of her sari to hide – to hide what? Blushes or simple delight?

But it seemed the modern girl was not so easily moved. Or – the thought struck him – perhaps she would not dislike so much being told she was pretty if the words had not come from – from a grandpapa.

However, he must not be put off. He had been lucky to have found someone who at least seemed to know more than a little about what went on at Oceanic College. He must work this mine down to its last half-kilo of ore.

So as the procession straggled on along the dark, deserted suburban road, managing now a single 'Autocracy murdabad' only at rare intervals, he produced a stream of innocuous queries about the college, its life and routines. Eventually he calculated his pretty little informant, whose name he learnt was Sarita Karatkar, ought to be lulled enough for it to be safe to approach again the heart of the matter.

'I was meaning to ask,' he said eventually, 'have you heard what has happened to young Bala? You know he is in hospital itself? In a deep coma? They are saying it is result of failed suicide.'

'Yes,' the girl said, concern swift in her voice. 'Yes, we were hearing something like that. So it is true?'

There was a note of plain doubt in her question. Ghote was quick to explore it.

'You are believing something else?' he asked carefully. 'That it is, for instance, just only heat stroke that has put him into hospital? Yes, sometimes coma is resulting from too much exposure to sun, and certainly it is damned hot by day just now, but the doctor at KEM Hospital was stating it was definitely due to taking some poison.'

'All the same,' Sarita Karatkar answered, the placard she was meant to be bravely holding aloft dipping slowly forward, 'I am knowing Bala quite well, however little I am liking him, and I would say he was not a person to be taking his own life.'

'No? Not even when he was realising police were on his heels. CIB fellows going to come from Delhi itself?'

The girl perked up, encouraged perhaps by an unexpected renewal of vigour in the shouts from the head of the procession.

'No, no,' she said. 'Not everybody is so afraid of you policewallas. Even if you are mistreating and torturing.'

'No, you must not be think– '

But, ahead, the shouts had faded abruptly into silence.

And the marchers were coming to a faltering halt, causing some of those in the rear to bump into those immediately in front of them. Others were stepping aside on to the broken-down edge of the road, half to see what was happening and half, it was plain, with the intention of slipping away. Questioning voices could be heard. But they were subdued and plainly uneasy.

Ghote left Sarita and walked on up till, in the light of the next distant street-lamp, he saw what had in fact brought about the tumbling halt.

A police havildar accompanied by a constable, was standing blocking the way. Each was armed with a long steel-tipped lathi, the big havildar twirling his with evident enjoyment, the constable, barely half his size, attempting to do the same. And, some thirty yards distant, just out of the pale lamplight there was another group of constables waiting.

Ghote felt a flicker of dismay. No police patrol on a quiet, deserted night road should be armed with lathis. They were issued only when trouble was expected. So had word of this demonstration got out? And had somebody who perhaps wanted the reputation of Oceanic College to be kept bright and shining contacted the local inspector and arranged for this unduly forceful police presence?

And plainly the big havildar, at least, was ready to use his lathi at the slightest opportunity.

'Get to hell out of this road,' he suddenly shouted now in the general direction of the morcha.

From the front rank one of the leaders, a tall young Sikh – turbaned, Ghote noted, but rebelliously without the uncut beard his religion enjoined – stepped forward, challenge in his bearing from jutting head to dancing heels.

'You are preventing our citizens' rights,' he shouted full in the big havildar's face.

It was just what the fellow wanted. A delighted gleam came into his eyes. He took a quick step back, raising his lathi high.

And down it came with a fearful whack.

Except that the moment it came into contact with the tall young Sikh's turban the whole weapon collapsed in a shower of rotten wood.

The constable evidently felt he had now to come to his senior's rescue. He raised his own lathi.

Ghote thought rapidly. Unless something was done there was going to be an ugly and unnecessary confrontation. Blood would be shed. Arrests made on doubtful charges of rowdyism.

He hurried forward, hauling from his pocket his ID.

'Havildar,' he said to the big fellow, still looking in dumb-ox amazement at the stub of lathi in his hands. 'I am a Crime Branch inspector. I have been keeping an eye on these youngsters in the course of inquiries. You can leave them to me now. They would be going off to bed in two – three minutes.'

The havildar glared back at him.

'Resume patrol,' Ghote snapped. 'That is an order.'

The fellow looked down at his heavy sandals. Then with a grunt he turned and moved off, resentment at being deprived of the entertainment he had evidently looked forward to plain in every hunched muscle of his back. His little companion followed like a rebuked puppy.

Ghote turned to the morcha, which had already coagulated into a small close-crowding clump. He suspected, in fact, that not a few from the rear ranks had long before doused their torches and made off.

'Enough,' he said. 'This has been enough now.'

He stood facing the leaders.

They glanced one to the other.

'No one was damn well seeing us anyhow,' one of them muttered.

They turned to go. But Sarita Karatkar was not so easily to be tamed.

'No,' she shouted, striding up. 'No, we are protesting against a full injustice. We have said we would march for one hour. We must do it.'

Ghote sighed.

He went up to her.

'Miss,' he said in a deliberately loud voice. 'You have been altogether most helpful with police inquiries. I am wanting to thank you.'

It was a nasty trick, he knew. But, as the girl herself had said, all was fair in love and war.

And the trick had the merit of working, too. With plainly hostile looks Sarita's fellow protestors began walking away from her into the thick, warm night.

Ghote gave her a brief smile.

'Tomorrow I would be here again,' he said. 'Perhaps I would be seeing you.'

4

Inspector Ghote had realised, as he had trailed back home to a mercifully sleeping family, that the next day he ought to get out to Oceanic College as early as classes there started. At 7.30, as elsewhere. It was likely, so he had gathered from Sarita Karatkar that Dr Shambu Bembalkar would be in his seat at that time, if not earlier.

'Princi is very much duty-bound, if nothing else,' she had said.

So he had had time only to learn from Ved that he had been elected captain of the Regals and to see Protima for no longer than it had taken to swallow a hasty breakfast.

One way not to be told what to do in my own home, he had thought with a dart of dark and not unpleasing humour, is to be hardly ever at home.

But the scene that greeted him at that distant academic institution was very different from the forlorn emptiness of the night before. After making his way past mile upon mile of industrial desolation, rolling mills, casting mills, soap factories, chemical factories, each lazily pouring out thickly oily smoke to settle sullenly on crouching areas of dank, mossed-over huts and shallow pools of deadened black water, he came upon a scene of lively, if disorganised, animation.

Stretching from near the door of the blockish white building of the college right out beyond the tall gates and along the footpath, there was a deep, milling line of young people together with a good many agitatedly discussing parents. Just inside the gate a big blackboard propped on its easel announced *Admissions to First Year BCom and FY BSc are full. Outsiders are requested not to see the Principal.*

The terse announcement affected him, oddly, almost as a personal blow. There was no question of himself, a police officer authorised to question, being considered an outsider from whom the college's Principal must at all costs be guarded. But he could not help thinking of the time, not so far off, when his Ved would be going to college. Would he himself, as the next academic year drew to its end, have to wait hour after hour outside St Xavier's Technical Institute on its admission day hoping to enter Ved? And perhaps be unlucky.

So after all had Protima been wise, wiser than she knew, in her taking advantage of that chance meeting with the wife of the Dean at Elphinston, outrageous though what she had done was? And did that mean that after all there was no need. . . ?

Resolutely he put out of his mind all the complex of thoughts that this seemed to be leading to. He had more important things to do. He must tackle without delay jealously protected Principal Bembalkar from whose locked chamber that question-paper had vanished.

He made his way rapidly past the long line of would-be students, with just the passing thought that there were far too many for them all to get places, whether in prized Bachelor of Commerce or Bachelor of Science courses or elsewhere. Doubtless, though, each one of the parents would be relieved of a certain number of rupees by way of a charge for an entry form. And in total those would make a nice sum for the college management.

Inside, he spotted an arrowed notice *Principal's Office* pointing to the wide staircase. He made his way briskly forwards, skirting a pair of angry parents being prevented from going up by a tall, green-uniformed, resplendently moustached security officer.

But, just as he had got past, a sudden grab at his shoulder brought him to a sharp halt.

He looked round. It was the security man.

'No persons to see Principal,' the fellow barked out.

Ghote gave him a cold glare.

'No persons,' he said, 'who are not police officers on duty. I am Inspector Ghote, Crime Branch CID.'

For a little it looked as if the lanky security officer was not going to accept his word. But after a moment of unchanged hostility he abruptly backed down.

'Sorry – sorry, Inspector sahib. Kindly go up.'

At the top of the broad stairway he found a long balcony looking down on to the college's inner courtyard. A little way along it there was a door marked *Principal*. He knocked and entered. Only to find Principal Shambu Bembalkar was protected yet further by an outer office in which there sat a secretary, Anglo-Indian to judge by her clothes, short skirt in severe black and a blouse in a fierce shade of red. Her name, *Mrs Angela Cooper*, was proclaimed in white-painted letters on a prominent little black triangular board on her desk. She looked up at him with a glance that was guardedly hostile.

'It is Inspector Ghote, Crime Branch CID,' he said, all the more briskly sharp from his encounter with the security officer below. 'I am wishing to see Dr Bembalkar.'

'Impossible.'

'Imposs– But, madam, I repeat, I am a police officer. A most serious crime has taken place here. There are urgent inquiries to be made.'

'Nevertheless you cannot see Principalji.'

He drew himself up.

'This is obstruction, nothing less. I must warn you, madam: it is an offence against Indian Penal Code, section 186.'

Mrs Cooper looked up at him, her bright red blouse puffed out with fighting determination. He saw her, suddenly, as a rakshas, a demon breathing fire, remembered from the tales of the boy God Krishna that his mother had endlessly told him.

'Inspector,' the rakshas said, flames jetting, 'if you are threatening with arrest I will take you to see Principalji. But let me warn you: you would not be welcome. Not welcome to Dr Bembalkar, and not at all welcome to Mrs Maya Rajwani.'

'Mrs Maya Rajwani?'

'The wife of Mr R. K. Rajwani, Rajwani Chemicals, and she is heading also Oceanic College Board of Trustees.'

Ghote began to understand.

Rajwani Chemicals was a familiar name. The firm was one of the more successful, up-and-coming enterprises in Bombay. One of its factories, indeed, had loomed out at him from the roadside not half an hour ago. Mr Rajwani would be a person of influence. By the sound of it, his wife was someone of almost equal influence. Interrupting her while she was in conference with the Principal of the college of which she was head trustee would be a considerably foolish action. And yet . . . If he was to find out just how that damned paper had been stolen and make a report that could be sent at top speed to the Centre he ought not to be stopped by any such obstacle.

'Very good, madam,' he said, however. 'There are many other inquiries that must be made. Perhaps I should come back after some time. When would Principal Bembalkar be free?'

Mrs Cooper remained inflexible.

'That is impossible to say.'

'But – But his conference with Mrs Rajwani cannot go on for ever. Kindly tell me what is the latest time it would last.'

'Inspector, I do not think you can be knowing what is the situation in the college just now.'

It sounded like an accusation.

Mrs Cooper looked at him with unvarying hostility. Fire at the lips of her rakshas' nostrils.

'There have been calls for the Principal's resignation,' she said.

Again Ghote thought he was getting a grasp of things.

'Ah, yes,' he replied. 'That morcha some students were taking out last night. I am very well knowing about that.'

'I do not think that is what is most worrying Principalji this morning,' Mrs Cooper answered. 'Say what you like, he would not be pushed from his seat by any student nonsense, however little he is able – '

She broke off. Ghote wondered briefly whether in the interests of discovering more about the man from whose chamber that question-paper had been stolen he should pursue this half-hint that the Principal was not an altogether strict administrator. But a possibly more worthwhile line of inquiry was there, too.

'Madam,' he said, 'what is it then that is more worrying to Principal Bembalkar this morning?'

He had put his question with such firmness that even this fire-breathing lady could hardly avoid giving him an answer.

'Inspector, I must not speak out of turn, but it is after all well known. Things have not been very easy in the college these past few months, and . . .'

Silence.

'Yes?' he said sharply.

Mrs Cooper, unexpectedly tamer, looked down at her typewriter, its dust cover already lifted off.

'Inspector, you must know yourself that university life is nothing like it was when, say, you must have been a student.'

'That is one hundred percent true, yes,' he said, thinking of the performance of the night before. 'One hundred and one percent. But what exactly is now the trouble?'

He thought he could detect a softening in the look he was given. Perhaps his hearty agreement about the deterioration in university life had helped.

'Oh, it is no worse here than at other colleges,' Mrs Cooper answered with a flick of returning pride. 'But, yes, our students are all the time taking advantage of Dr Bembalkar. He is such a true scholar also. So he is not always the best person for keeping discipline. And now that this paper has been stolen from his very chamber, when it was his sacred duty to guard it, well, there have been demands from some politicians and from some senior colleagues here also for resignation.'

'And he is resisting same?'

'No, no, Inspector.'

'No? You are saying he is after all wanting to quit?'

Mrs Cooper actually smiled now. It was a smile of confidentiality.

'Between you and me, Inspector,' she said, 'Dr Bembalkar would be only too pleased to leave his seat.'

'But then what-all is his meeting with Mrs Maya Rajwani about? If the trustees are wanting him to resign and he is wanting also, where is the problem?'

Mrs Cooper sighed.

'Inspector,' she said, 'you do not understand the difficulties that are facing Dr Bembalkar. You do not at all understand. Others are wanting him to resign, yes. But the trustees – Well, it is Mrs Rajwani herself, she is very, very anxious for him to stay.'

Ghote pondered.

'But why is that?' he asked at last, still puzzled.

'Inspector, I cannot say.'

He thought, however, from the tone of her reply that probably she could say. He even wondered whether he should press her to answer. But, partly because he suspected that he would find this not at all easy, and partly because he was not sure whether what he might learn would have a bearing on his inquiries, he let it slide.

And in any case, as if worried that she had already said too much, Mrs Cooper was quick now to add to her ambiguous statement.

'You see,' she said, 'Dr Bembalkar would very much like to have more time for his studies. He is writing a very, very important book.'

'Oh, yes? It is to state what should be done in our Indian universities?'

'No, no, no. It is *Hamlet*.'

'*Hamlet*? What is this?'

The Principal's guardian rakshas shot him a fiery look.

'It is Shakespeare's play, Inspector,' she said. 'The world's most famous. Principalji is making a very highly important study of same.'

Ghote inwardly cursed himself. Although *Macbeth* was the only one of

Shakespeare's plays he had ever been acquainted with, he knew the existence of *Hamlet* perfectly well. He gathered his wits.

'So Principal Bembalkar is writing his book on that famous play,' he said, hoping to blot out his error. 'Please, when it will be released? I must try to obtain one copy.'

'But it will not be coming out for some time. In fact, I can tell you Dr Bembalkar has not yet begun some actual writing. There is much, much research needed.'

Ghote could not quite see how there could be room for all that much research on what was after all just one play. But perhaps *Hamlet* was so famous because it was altogether longer than *Macbeth*, a nine-nights' affair like the Ramayana plays. But he was not going to risk antagonising his useful source of information again by making any such comment. He had developed a notion that the rakshas, for all her ferocity, had 'a soft corner' for Principal Bembalkar. And it might well be of considerable use to him to know as much as possible about the man. After all, the way that the question-paper had been spirited out of his locked chamber was a total mystery. The man's personality might well lead to solving that riddle.

'Tell me,' he said, 'is Dr Bembalkar. . . ? Well, in my college days we had some professors who were – you know what it is they are always saying – well, absent-minded.'

But he had failed to take into account the soft corner he had guessed at.

'No, no,' Mrs Cooper said, rage belching out once more. 'No one should say that about Dr Bembalkar. He is a very, very great scholar, altogether too understanding and kind-hearted to be very firm in punishing students. But he is not at all absent-minded. Not at all.'

She gave Ghote a new glare.

Sadly he acknowledged that, for the time being at least, he had lost the art of standing unscathed amid rakshah's breath. Time to cut his losses.

'But I must not be chit-chatting here,' he said with as much decisiveness as he could summon up. 'There is much of work to be done. Yes, very much of work.'

'Yes, yes,' Mrs Cooper said with some eagerness. 'Go now, and come back after some time. It is no use you standing here, as Principalji is often saying, like the poor cat in the adage.'

Outside on the wide veranda, Ghote found himself puzzling hard about that last remark. *The poor cat in the adage.* The words were familiar. They even seemed to be hovering just short of the forefront of his mind, although he could have sworn he had not heard the expression for years.

And then he got it. A jagged lightning-flash of recall.

It came precisely from that one play of Shakespeare's he had studied, years ago at the end of his schooldays, *Macbeth*. He remembered the curious English word 'adage' being explained to the class, and how, although he had written a careful note at the time, he had, even immediately afterwards, been somehow unable to recall what it meant. Nor had he ever got it properly lodged in his mind. Time and again he had had to return to the note he had made, until at last, school left behind, he had ceased to need to know.

Even now, tease his brain how he might, he could not at all remember.

So how did the expression apply to him at this moment? There had seemed to be an underlying hint of criticism in Mrs Cooper's use of it. Had that been there? And, if it had, what was he being criticised for? What?

At last, with an unhappy internal shrug, he abandoned the hunt.

5

Ghote had told the fire-spurting rakshas that he had work to do. He must get on with it. Only . . . Only he was momentarily at a loss as to just where this work was actually to be found. He felt a new dart of exasperation. Here he was, determined to show those CBI wallas that there was anyhow one officer in Bombay able to get things done, and at every point what was he meeting but checks and difficulties.

Perhaps, he thought suddenly, that was what an adage was. A sort of very cunning trap, something that created more and more difficulties the harder you tried to escape from it. Was that it? Something that added coil after trapping coil, added and added. An addage.

It did not revive an exact memory of the word he had learnt, or failed to learn, at school. But certainly here difficulties had been added and added to his task from the very start. Even that security man –

Wait. Yes, by God, there was somewhere to break out of it. That fellow down in the entrance hall ought to know about locks and keys and who had them and who could get at them. It was his duty itself to know. So a one hundred percent good talk with Mr Security Officer. Now.

He went stamping down the stairway, brushing past books-clutching students coming up, grim with renewed determination.

The fellow was still just inside the wide double doors, busy examining a young man's identity card, glowering at it as if it was bound to be somehow a forgery.

'You there,' Ghote addressed him. 'You are one of College's security officers, yes?'

The tall fellow lifted his head, huge moustache rising on his lip.

'I am sole and only security officer, Inspector,' he said. 'One Amar Nath by name.'

'Very good. Drop all that card nonsense. I am wanting to talk. In private. And now only.'

For a single instant Amar Nath looked down at the identity card he was holding, as if reluctant to allow it to be authentic. But then he tossed it back to the student in front of him and turned to Ghote.

'Inspector,' he said, 'One cup of tea would be good, yes? At chaikhana opposite I am well known.'

Ghote did not altogether like the idea of sitting down over a friendly cup of tea. He had seen his questioning of the security officer as being an altogether more formal affair. A desk, at which he himself was sitting, upright and forceful, and the fellow standing in front of him. At attention.

However, there was no desk to hand, nor anywhere at his disposal where a desk might be found. And, in any case, he might learn more in friendly circumstances than by any amount of sharp interrogation.

Or was this going to prove just one more entangling coil in the adage, the addage?

'Very well,' he said, with rapid inward resignation. 'Let's go. But, mind, I do not have time for just only gup-shup.'

'No, Inspector, no, no.'

Briskly Amar Nath led the way out past the long line of applicants for First Year places – they did not seem to have made any progress – through the college gate and across the road to where there was a tea-shop, blotted out the night before when it had been unlit and its shutter had been down. Despite its name, Paris Hotel, just to be made out in faded yellow letters on a board above the shutter, it did not look at all high-class.

Inside, it seemed no better. There was a strong smell of over-boiled tea. The blue painted walls, on which three or four out-of-date calendars hung limply, were peeling in places. Nor did the handful of students at the plastic-topped tables, some leaning close in confidential chat, one or two others reading in morose solitude, look very interested in the cooling half-cups of tea in front of them.

But at Amar Nath's arrival the proprietor, gloomily perusing a big black account-book at the entrance, showed welcome signs of life. He banged the domed bell beside him with vigour. From the back a boy in scanty shirt and drooping khaki half-pants emerged, took one look at Amar Nath and at once proceeded to give the best of the unoccupied tables a good flicking-over with the stained cloth from over his shoulder.

'Tea, Proprietor sahib,' Amar Nath said boomingly. 'One double omelet, toast.'

He turned to Ghote.

'Inspector, you will take also?'

'Just only tea,' Ghote said, seeing his business-like scenario already being badly eroded.

So, as soon as they had seated themselves and the boy had banged two smeary glasses of water down in front of them, he leant forward and addressed the security man's expansively moustached face.

'You must be knowing what for I am here,' he said. 'It is this theft from your Principal's office of a question-paper, Statistical Techniques.'

'Yes, yes. That Bala Chambhar is one bloody anti-social.'

'So much I am already knowing. But what I am needing to find out is how did the fellow get into the Principal's chamber? It was locked, isn't it?'

'Oh, yes, Inspector,' Amar Nath happily replied in his broad Punjabi accent. 'Locked, locked.'

'Then how was Bala Chambhar getting in?'

Amar Nath looked puzzled. Plainly this was something he had yet to ask himself.

'Don't know, Inspector. But if I had caught him I would break his bones, I can tell you.'

'Yes, yes. But that would not help in knowing how he was getting into a room that was altogether locked. What about the windows? I have not been inside, but it is up on the first floor, yes? So could this Bala have climbed in?'

Amar Nath sat and thought. The boy brought their two cups of tea. Ghote noted that, unasked, they had been given Specials, teaspoons in the saucers of their extra large cups.

Amar Nath poured a splashy quantity of the milky brown liquid into his saucer and raised it to slurp.

Ghote put out a hand and steered the saucer back to the table top.

'Could Bala Chambhar have climbed into Principal's chamber?' he repeated.

'No.'

'No? You are certain?'

'Yes, yes, Inspector. I am seeing those windows in my mind. There are two only. Side by side. And the wall underneath, smooth-smooth.'

'So how do you think the boy got in? That Mrs Angela Cooper, is she always outside at her desk there? I am thinking she would not so easily desert her post.'

Amar Nath, for all his slowness, at once caught on to the implication of this.

He gave a loud guffaw.

'Is there almost all the damn time, yes,' he said. 'Would like to get into Princi pants. Married or not married, child or not child.'

Ghote decided not to respond.

'So with Mrs Cooper outside and no way to climb up to the windows how did Bala Chambhar get hold of that question-paper?' he repeated.

'Easy, Inspector.'

'Easy?'

Ghote felt a jab of annoyance.

'Even those Anglo-Indian women got to eat,' Amar Nath answered. 'Keep up their strength for hanky-pankies.'

'I see. Mrs Cooper goes to eat at some time, and it was while she was away that Bala Chambhar was taking the question-paper.'

Amar Nath gave a massive shrug.

'Looks like.'

'But Dr Bembalkar, isn't it that he would lock his chamber door? When there are exam papers inside? He must be knowing that there have been leakages at other colleges.'

'Oh, yes, Inspector, lock up and lock up he would. What is my duty after all? To make sure what should be locked is locked. And this I can be telling. Princi may be all sorts of a damn fool, but he is very-very keen on lockings-up. Each time I pass by that office when there is no one there I am going in and checking his door itself. Duty is duty. And never one time am I finding same unlocked.'

Ghote thought for a little. The boy came up with Amar Nath's double omelet. It looked as leathery and greasy as he had guessed and so small it seemed doubtful that two eggs besides a sprinkling of green chilli could have gone to its making.

'Toast,' Amar Nath yelled at the boy. 'Where my damn toast?'

'Coming, sahib, coming-coming.'

'Listen,' Ghote said when Amar Nath had turned to his omelet and begun tearing it apart. 'You are saying and saying Principal Bembalkar is a damn fool. But, if he is always so certain in locking his office, what about is he so much of a damn fool?'

Amar Nath gave a healthy belch.

'Everything,' he said cheerfully. 'All the bloody same those professors and their question-papers this and question-papers that. Do nothing, say plenty. Princi, Dean Potdar, all all. That Dr Mrs Gulabchand, sitting there and saying nothing, but all the time pushing and pushing to get where she is wanting. And look at that Potdar. Little fat owl, with all those daughters he has and none-none married. Dean is meant to be keeping order, no? But what is he doing? Making nasty remarks about each and every one of the others from Princi down, but never at all keeping those damn boys in their place. Or those girls. Worse than boys, I say. What they are needing is one damn good touch of a belt. I would give it, girl or boy.'

For a moment Ghote allowed himself to wonder whether Amar Nath's solution to the problem of discipline might not be . . .

'All the same,' Amar Nath banged on. 'Not one of them any good for any damn thing.'

He jerked forward and peered suddenly into his tea-cup.

'No,' he said. 'Not true. One only is any good. You are knowing Professor Kapur?'

'No,' Ghote said, wondering why he should.

'Is teaching astrology. Damn good fellow. He keeps those brats in order. And he will tell even a security officer what is waiting in future.'

A professor of astrology, and at a college of Bombay University itself. Ghote felt a sense of insult. Yes, colleges in less up-to-date parts of the country had astrology professors, and there were astrologers in plenty in seemingly equally up-to-date Delhi who, if newspaper gossip was true, advised even the most illustrious figures. But in Bombay? What sort of a place had he come to?

But then, he thought, Oceanic College must be hanging on to Bombay University only by the skins of its teeth. And if it was, what kind of an efficient officer was its one and only security man? Could what he had claimed about doing his duty and making sure locks were locked be just only boastings? Was the Principal's chamber, in fact, always safely locked in his absence?

He decided the time had come to take a tough line.

He stood up.

'Now listen to me,' he said. 'That question-paper Bala Chambhar was stealing may seem to you to be only some nonsense of your professors. But it is damn important to some people. People who can make one hell of a lot of troubles if they are not getting results they are wanting. So, enough of stating you are doing this and doing that as your bounden duty, and tell me, no shadow of any lie, how many times have you found that Principal's chamber unlocked?'

It was plain he had succeeded in knocking some respect into the big Punjabi. But the answer he got did not advance him a single inch.

'Inspector, I swear it by each and every god. That room has never been unlocked when there was no one in. I swear it.'

'Very well. But I am hoping for your sake you are telling truth only.'

He turned and marched out.

But he was all too conscious that his talk with the security officer, though it had brought him its share of information, useful or not, had not been the escape from his toils he had hoped for. It had left him just where he was in his self-set task of showing the men from Delhi that there were better detectives in India than the ones who air-dashed here and there at a word from somebody up above.

6

Ghote could not prevent himself feeling, as once again he approached Mrs Cooper's desk, that somehow he would find himself yet more caught up like a cat entangled in a fishing net adage. Nevertheless he addressed the red-bloused rakshas with determined optimism.

'Principalji is able to see me now?'

'No, Inspector. He is not.'

The confirmation of his uneasy feeling did nothing to lessen it.

'But you have told I am here?'

'No, Inspector.'

'But – '

'Mrs Rajwani is still inside.'

'She is here so long? You are certain?'

'Inspector, I am all the time in my seat.'

Would he ever get to see this man, his key witness? Should he insist now? Shout even?

Then second thoughts prevailed. After all, he did not need to see the Principal at exactly this time. He could certainly wait a little longer. A little. And there was someone else he probably ought to see.

'Madam,' he said, 'it is most important I should also be speaking with Dean Potdar. I have many, many inquiries to make.'

'Very well, Inspector. Dean's office is three doors from here itself.'

He had had at the moment he proposed seeing the Dean no exact idea what he might find out from him. Indeed, he had half-expected, as a blow to be flinched from, that Mrs Cooper would again compare him to a poor cat, however little he could fathom why she had done so in the first place.

But, it seemed, he was not in making this request cat-like. No new coils of the adage were ready to flick down on him.

Then, walking slowly as he could past the doors that separated Principal from Dean, an idea came to him. Just in time. If Bala Chambhar was as much of an anti-social as Amar Nath had claimed and as even the girl in the green sari, Sarita, had agreed, then the boy would surely have come to the notice of the Dean, and on more than one occasion. So it was possible that the Dean might know something about him that might provide a clue as to how he could have stolen that question-paper from what seemed to be an ever-locked room.

The Dean, he found, also had a secretary in an outer office. But she was no sort of a rakshas, just a large middle-aged lady sitting at her desk comfortably knitting. He gave her his name and asked to see the Dean immediately. She pressed a switch on her intercom box, and a moment later he found himself confronting Dr Potdar.

The Dean was a small man, looking older than Ghote had expected. He was sitting, for all the steady heat of Bombay's June, in jacket, tie and academic gown, behind a desk awash with papers. He had a round little face with across his pudgy little nose a pair of round-rimmed gold pince-nez, and, just visible at the desk's edge, a round little stomach protruded. All in all he did not, Ghote thought, seem like the father of so many daughters whom Amar Nath had described so contemptuously. But in such matters you could never tell.

'Well, Inspector – Inspector Ghote, is it? – what is it I can do for you?'

'Sir, I am making inquiries. There has been a theft. A certain question-paper in Statis– '

'Inspector, do you think I do not know about that?' Behind his pince-nez Dean Potdar's eyes twinkled with what was surely malice. 'Every single person in this college has been talking of nothing else ever since it came out that young Chambhar was selling that question-paper through entire Bombay.'

'Yes, sir, of course,' Ghote replied, the notion that he was being made to look stupid prickling sharply through his head.

He drew in a breath.

'It is, in fact, this boy, Bala Chambhar, I am wanting to discuss,' he said with some sharpness. 'You see, sir, it is not so far clear how he was actually managing to commit that offence, and as he is in a state of deep coma we are not able to question.'

'No, Inspector, I can see that even the Bombay police with all their scientific methods, or other more – shall we say? – brutal techniques, would scarcely be able to interrogate a boy in that state. And the coma is, did you say, deep? Profound, I believe is the medical expression.'

Ghote was tempted to reply yet more sharply that he had heard of the medical term. But caution stopped him.

Why not, he thought, allow this fat little professor-type to think he was successfully taunting and teasing a thoroughly stupid police inspector? Then the fellow might say things, for example, about Principal Bembalkar who according at least to Amar Nath he despised and disliked, that he would not otherwise let out. And the more he himself knew about the man from whose chamber that paper had mysteriously been spirited the better.

'Profound coma, yes, yes,' he accepted Dean Potdar's correction in a tone of fawning gratitude.

'Yes,' the Dean went on, twinkling yet more cheerfully. 'So poor young Chambhar is in a state of profound coma. Did they tell you at the hospital what his chances were?'

'I have not visited hospital myself personally,' Ghote answered, striving to give the impression that this would be something almost beyond his powers. 'They were sending officers from what we are calling the Central Bureau of Investigation itself. I am just only clearing up the one or two missing points.'

'I see. But these CBI officers – I have heard of that institution, you know, Inspector – what were they reporting about young Chambhar's state?'

'Oh, sir, that he was most likely to expire without regaining any of consciousness.'

'I see. Poor chap, poor chap.'

'You are feeling very great sympathy for him?' Ghote asked, pouring on the perplexity. 'When he is the proven thief of that question-paper?'

Dean Potdar gave a puffy little sigh.

'Well, I am not denying that Chambhar was a bad lad, Inspector. Very much a bad lad, I am sorry to say. Many a time I have had to have him up for some offence or another. Why, he was standing in front of me only a few days ago, just where you are now. But, my dear fellow, you should not keep standing yourself. Please sit. No need of formality with me.'

Ghote pulled back one of the three hard chairs drawn up in front of the Dean's desk, and took care to perch himself awkwardly on its very edge.

'Please, sir,' he said, 'what for were you just now calling Bala Chambhar as one poor chap?'

The Dean gave a sharp little smile.

'Precisely because he was poor, Inspector,' he replied.

'Poor, sir? I am not at all understanding.'

'Poor, Inspector. Indigent, impecunious, impoverished, penurious.'

Ghote contrived to blink.

'In short, Inspector, the boy was one of those claiming the Reserved Seats for the Harijan community. In fact, to put it bluntly, he should really not have attempted to acquire a college education. The groundwork was not there. Not at all. But one had to give him credit for some persistence. Which was why I had not resorted to the utmost sanction.'

'And what is that, please?'

The eyes behind the pince-nez redoubled their teasing twinkling.

'Terminating his career here, Inspector. In other words, giving him, as you might say, the boot.'

'Oh, yes, sir, yes. That was most good of you.'

Dean Potdar leant back in his chair, as far as his rotund little frame permitted.

'So what precisely have you come to me for, Inspector?'

Ghote gave a little cough.

'Sir,' he said, 'it is this question of when and how exactly the said Bala Chambhar was abstracting – ' he paused as if he had not been quite sure whether he had used the right word. Should he have risked 'subtracting'? '– was abstracting that question-paper from the Principal's office. I was wondering if you could help me in that.'

'Help you? Well, I don't see that I can. I imagine it will become clear even to – that it will become clear to you sooner or later.'

'Yes, sir, yes. But it is a matter of sooner, please. I am having to make report to the CBI itself, the Central Bureau . . .'

'I see. Well then, shall we go over the circumstances? I have no doubt that, once you have got those straight in your mind, Inspector, all will become plain.'

'Yes, sir.'

'So, that paper was stolen on – let me see – why, yes, on Monday. It seems longer with all the brouhaha there has been. All the hulla-gulla, Inspector. And it must surely have been during the luncheon hour that the deed was done. The papers had arrived only that morning, under strict guard, and, if they were being sold all over the city on Tuesday, then Monday it would have been. Now, the only time, so far as I am aware, that there is no one either in the Principal's chamber itself or in the outer office is for some few minutes after one o'clock. Principal Bembalkar customarily lunches between one and two – poor man he has had little appetite these past few days – and I believe his secretary, the beauteous Mrs Cooper, generally takes a short break earlier so that she is present during at least the latter half of the period the Principal is absent.'

He gave Ghote a little playful smile.

'You see, Inspector, already we are narrowing things down. No. No, I am wrong. On Monday, I remember now, Bembalkar took his luncheon early.'

'Yes, sir?'

Was this another piece of his teasing, Ghote wondered. Or was there actually something of value he was about to learn? Because it had looked as if the Dean had truly at just that moment hit on something he had not thought of before.

'Yes, Inspector, there was an incident on Monday. Something that had quite been put out of my head by the subsequent brouhaha.'

'An incident?' Ghote prompted carefully, afraid the Dean might be too happy teasing his stupid police officer to come out with what he had been about to say.

'Yes, Inspector, you see, there is a certain lecturer in the college, a lecturer in English Literature, by the name of Furtado, Victor Furtado. A person – I am bound to say this, Inspector – not entirely satisfactory as a member of our academic staff. Now, somehow he has recently contrived to get more than usually on the wrong side of his classes. So last Monday a few of the more daring spirits took it on themselves to blacken Furtado's face.'

'They resorted to abuses, sir?'

'No, no, Inspector. It was literally, as we say, that they had decided on this face-blackening. With some tarry substance, as I understand it. And the place they chose for this ceremony was the courtyard below the veranda here. The affair, in fact, caused so much hilarity – and I dare say Furtado emitted a scream or two – that, I understand, the Principal himself came out to remonstrate. To no effect, I am sorry to say. In fact, he was so distressed, poor fellow, that he took an early luncheon. I myself saw him arrive for it at about half-past twelve. So, do you begin to see what must have happened, Inspector?'

Ghote had seen. The CBI men in their report had got it wrong. Principal Bembalkar's office had been without anyone present not just between 1300 hours and 1330 hours, as they had said, but from some time after, say, half-past twelve onwards. So if someone had another key, or . . .

He almost jumped up there and then to hurry back to the Principal's office and see what a few sharp questions there might reveal.

But caution prevailed. It might still pay off to keep Dean Potdar thinking he had a thickly stupid police officer to deal with. So, wait a moment more and make sure it was not evident he had zoomed already to the end of the Dean's trail.

'No, sir,' he said, shaking his head like a bemused bandicoot. 'I am sorry I am not at all seeing.'

'Why, man, it is simple. For once the Principal's office was unguarded for a considerable time. From, let us say, 12.30 until at least 1.15. That is when the theft must have occurred, Inspector. Just then. That is when our friend Chambhar must have taken that question-paper.'

Except, Ghote thought, there is still the business of how Chambhar spirited the paper out of the Principal's locked chamber. But he kept that thought to himself.

'Oh, yes, sir, yes,' he said. 'I think you have found the answer, definitely. Thank you very much. You have been altogether helpful. I must now see Principalji at once. To obtain confirmation.'

Retaining to the last his stupid police officer persona, he made his way, grinning and stumbling, out of the room.

7

Excitement beginning to bubble up, Ghote hurried back along to the Principal's office. To find rakshas Mrs Cooper breathing new and hotter fire.

'No,' she said the moment he stepped in. 'Principalji cannot see you.'

'He is even now still talking with Mrs Rajwani? After so long?'

He found that hard to believe. Even impossible. And he recalled the 'soft corner' he suspected the rakshas had for the one she guarded.

He stood for a moment listening hard. From the far side of the plain wood door of the Principal's chamber there was only a deep silence.

'I am not at all hearing voices inside,' he said.

'Inspector, do you think the Principal of a college of Bombay University is conducting his conversations as if he was a fish-woman shouting and calling?'

There could be only one answer in face of that. Despite misgivings.

He strode over to the much-guarded door and thrust it open.

And there, as he had really expected, he saw no one except, sitting chin in hands behind a wide, well-polished teak table, staring glumly in front of him, the man who could only be Principal Shambu Bembalkar.

Big and broad-shouldered, he was wearing, as had Dean Potdar, a tweed jacket and a tie, even in the June heat which the grumbling air-conditioner in the nearer of the room's two windows was doing little to make more endurable. Only missing was the academic gown with which the Dean had dignified his tubby frame.

At Ghote's crashing entrance he had hardly looked up over the thick-rimmed spectacles that hid much of his long, heavily jowled face.

The very lack of an angry explosion gave Ghote pause.

'It is Principal Bembalkar?' he said, more quietly than he had intended.

Wearily the Principal seemed to pull himself together.

'Yes. What – What is it you are wanting? I am sorry, who did my secretary say you were?'

Ghote ignored the fact that Mrs Cooper had not at all announced him.

'I am by name Inspector Ghote, Crime Branch CID,' he said. 'Dr Bembalkar, I must speak with you most urgently concerning this theft of the Statistical Techniques question-paper.'

Dr Bembalkar heaved a long sigh and gropingly extracted a pipe from a long rack at his elbow.

'Yes,' he said. 'Yes, I gathered yesterday from the officers from Delhi that someone else would want to see me.'

He put the pipe into his mouth, but then at once removed it.

'Do take a pew,' he said. 'And what . . . What can I tell you? It was Inspector . . . ?'

'Inspector Ghote, sir.'

Ghote had rapidly come to the conclusion that the way to learn anything from this apparently numbed figure would be to go very slowly. So he contented himself with no more than that repetition of his name.

A silence fell.

'So what is it you want from me?' the Principal said at last, apparently realising he had someone on the other side of his wide table.

'It is this, sir. You are aware, no doubt, that the student from this college who was found to be selling copies of the missing paper, one Chambhar by name, Bala Chambhar, is at present lying in the KEM Hospital in a state of coma and is unable to be questioned. But in Delhi they are very, very anxious that this whole matter should be brought to the light down to its last detail.'

He decided now to let a new silence develop. For one thing from the dullness of the eyes behind the Principal's heavy-rimmed spectacles it looked as if he was having difficulty taking in much that was said to him, and for another he hoped that if he himself were to say nothing the Principal would at last volunteer some useful facts.

But why was he so beaten down and bemused?

Yet it seemed facts were not going to be forthcoming. All the Principal did was to put his pipe back in his mouth and suck at it emptily.

After a while the sound became so irritating that Ghote was the one who felt impelled to speak.

'Sir, the problem is this. Your chamber is said to be locked whenever you are not inside itself, and you are possessing its sole and only key. So when and how could the boy Bala have got in here? Delhi itself is wanting to know.'

Suck, suck, suck at the empty pipe.

But now Ghote steeled himself once again not to respond, however long he had to endure the sound. The silence across the wide gleaming teak table grew.

And grew.

Suck.

Suck, suck.

Suck, suck, suck.

Suck.

Till, again, it was Ghote's nerve that broke.

'Sir,' he said, 'I am understanding from Dean Potdar that last Monday when this theft must have taken place you had occasion to come out from this chamber to rebuke some student rag or prank.'

'Yes,' the Principal did at least answer. 'Yes, a disgraceful scene.'

He sighed, almost groaned.

'You know, Inspector – Inspector Khote, was it?'

'Ghote, sir. Inspector Ghote.'

'Oh, yes, of course. Forgive me. But, you know, Inspector, the student today is a very different young person from when I was in college myself, or even I suppose when you were. They demand, you know, even the right to cheat. The right to cheat. You can imagine the difficulties we have in invigilating examinations. It is nothing short of a nightmare. A nightmare.'

'Yes, sir, I am sure that it must be such,' Ghote said quickly, before that suck-sucking could start again. 'And, sir, you must also have to take very much of precaution to guard question-papers before exams are beginning. And that is why – '

But Dr Bembalkar, as if Ghote had not intervened at all, stumbled into heavy speech once more.

'I can understand their feelings, however. Yes, their situation is considerably different from what it was in my day. Yes. Then an examination was a test, a test of one's abilities. One read all the syllabus, putting in as much effort as one was capable of. Then one wrote the exam, and one abided by the result. But now . . . Now these young people *expect* to succeed.'

For a moment the stem of the pipe hovered near his mouth, and Ghote searched desperately for something to say to avert a new spell of silence and sucking.

However, he need not have worried. More bullock-cart creaking speech came from the pipeless lips.

'An exam to the youth today – and we in India are gravely to blame for this – an exam to them is, one might say, no more than a necessary step on their path to their chosen profession, or the profession parents have chosen for them. It is necessary for them that they should pass. That they should put the obstacle behind them. It is no more than something that has to be, in whatsoever way, surmounted. So to them the word cheat has a very different complexion than it did in my young day. Then it was a sin, no less. Now it means something more like a ruse, a necessary and even commendable ruse.'

Ghote, who in his time at Elphinston had felt the examinations he faced were, like those of Principal Bembalkar's youth, tests of how much he had learnt and nothing else, absorbed the meaning of this ponderous lecture.

And felt a spasm of irritation that it had come between him and finding the answer to the mystery he had come to solve.

Hastily he made an effort to get back to what he had been asking when Dr Bembalkar's long and gloomy diatribe had begun.

'Sir,' he said, 'I was inquiring about the incident that was occurring below your veranda on the day the paper was taken itself.'

The Principal fell back into thought. But the pipe, mercifully, stayed reasonably far from his mouth.

'Yes,' he said at last. 'I was hearing some sort of a disturbance. Noise, shouts and so forth. Eventually I went out to see what was causing such a fearful hullabaloo. I am afraid I found one of my lecturers, indeed a lecturer in my own discipline, English Literature, was being – I can only say – attacked. I addressed those responsible. Gentlemen, I said, as your senior I beg you to cease this unseemly business. But they took little notice. Yes, little notice.'

He lapsed again into silence, and before Ghote could think of any way of stopping it the pipe once more got to his mouth. But he sucked at it only twice. Then, with the stem still between his lips, he gave a long sigh and resumed.

'The truth, I am sorry to have to say, is that I am sometimes not as strict with delinquent students as perhaps I ought to be. Like Shakespeare's Prince Hamlet, Inspector, I am often too much sicklied o'er with the pale cast of thought.'

Briefly Ghote thought about those poetic words. They certainly seemed to say something he had himself sometimes half-thought. Yes, certainly the – what it was? – pale cast of thought could sickly over decisions to act. It happened to himself, no doubt about it. Protima, and his decision to . . . But he must stick to the matter in hand.

He straightened himself up, determined not to be diverted again.

'Sir,' he said, 'I must ask this. When you were attempting to deal with that disturbance is it possible that you left your door open behind you? Was Mrs Cooper present at that time, sir? I think she must have been somehow absent. Otherwise she would have told you what was occurring, rather than you yourself just only hearing the row. So, sir, can it have been at that short moment that Bala Chambhar was slipping into this room?'

But this question Dr Bembalkar answered without giving himself any time for thought.

'No, Inspector,' he said. 'Mrs Cooper was absent at that time, yes. It was her lunch period. But what you have proposed would nevertheless be quite impossible.'

'Impossible? But, sir – '

'No, you see, Inspector, that ragging party – and I fear that is too weak a term for it – was led by just this young man Chambhar.'

'It was led by Bala Chambhar?'

'Yes, yes, Inspector. I have had occasion to rebuke the young man more than once. So I clearly recognised him. I even called to him by name, though without any success I regret to say.'

Principal Bembalkar went back at that to his blank sucking at his pipe. But now Ghote was oblivious of the sound. He had too much to think about.

The point is, he inwardly addressed himself, however much it is now seeming Bala Chambhar is off the hooks, that question-paper nevertheless disappeared from this chamber itself, and next day Bala Chambhar was selling copies to each and every BCom student he could find. So there must be some link-up between whoever was that thief and Bala. What it is? And – this is something else – Principal Bembalkar is not happy. He is at this moment looking one hundred percent like a man with very much of worry. What is the cause of that? It may be just only that he is wanting to resign and for some reason that very influential lady, Mrs Rajwani, is not letting. But also he has not at all been good at answering my questions about this selfsame disappearance. No, there is something more to be got here. Definitely.

He gave a sharp little cough.

'Dr Bembalkar,' he said, 'can you, despite what you have told, in any way account for Bala Chambhar selling that paper, stolen from this room itself? How was that happening? How?'

The Principal's head jerked up. But he made no immediate reply.

For a moment Ghote thought of repeating what he had said, even more forcefully. But then it struck him that silence, after all, might yet be his best weapon.

He sat still and waited.

The minutes passed, marked out by the regular sucks at the Principal's pipe. One minute. Two, certainly. Had they stretched to three?

Suddenly Dr Bembalkar gave a loud groan.

'Inspector.'

Ghote said nothing.

'Inspector, there is something I should tell you.'

Still Ghote said not a word.

'Inspector, on that Monday, that black, black Monday, I was remiss. More than remiss. I was derelict in my duty. Inspector, after I had attempted to deal with that disturbance I was so – so upset in myself that I decided to take my lunch early. To settle my nerves. And – And, Inspector, I walked away from this chamber and left in its door my keys.'

8

Ghote's first reaction, emerging from the Principal's office on to the long balcony outside, was one of triumph. The cat in the adage had scratched and bitten its way to freedom. He had found the answer to a mystery that had defeated the men from the Central Bureau of Investigation itself.

But then, as he began to think about the report he would write and how he would have to suppress direct criticism of the CBI wallas but at the same time make it clear that he had bested them, he saw that his task was, in fact, by no means over. Yes, he had solved the mystery of how that question-paper could have been spirited out of a locked room. But at the same time Principal Bembalkar had made it clear beyond doubt that Bala Chambhar had been actively taking part in that rag when his chamber was unlocked and its guardian rakshas absent. So, until it was established how the stolen paper had actually got into Bala's hands his report would have to remain unwritten.

And finding that link was not going to be all plain sailings, he thought. Perhaps those Delhi fellows had not been checked by such a minor obstacle after all.

Was the poor cat yet more tangled up in that adage?

What inquiries could he make now that the CBI wallas had not? Bala Chambhar, lying almost as if dead in the KEM Hospital, was an immovable obstacle between himself and the truth, just as he had been for the CBI men. Without a clue from the boy, some hint which, had he been in a cell, could have been tricked out of him, or threatened out of him, or even got out of him with slapping or worse – those fellows from the Centre would not have hesitated – there was no telling who to see here in the college, what to ask.

There was nowhere to turn. Yes, no way out of the thick, twining branches and creepers making up, one after the other, his adage.

For a moment he contemplated simply giving up for the time being, trusting to luck or to something, to anything to give him some lead of some sort eventually. In the meanwhile he could go home, take rest.

Or, no, he could do what he had already put off doing for longer than he had meant to. He could get the business of beating Protima over and done with. He could make it plain once and for all who was master.

Yes, he would go back home and at least achieve one thing.

Or . . .

Well, perhaps he ought just to go to the KEM Hospital first and check on Bala Chambhar. The boy might have come out of his coma. Or he might, perhaps, have risen out of coma enough to have murmured some words. And, after all, if he had just done that, surely those words would very likely be concerned with what he had poisoned himself over, what would have been obsessing him at the time. And a nurse or a doctor might have heard them, remembered them.

Yes, it was definitely his duty to go, not back home, but to the hospital.

Getting there, however, was not as easy as all that, thanks to the traffic-jostling distance between far-out Oceanic College and Acharya Dhonde Marg, or King Edward Road as it had been when he had first come to Bombay, hence the King Edward Memorial Hospital. And when at last he got down to the southern heart of the city the mere bulk of the huge hospital almost proved too much for him.

It was not until well into the afternoon, long after he had abandoned his intolerably over-heated vehicle in the big dusty compound in front of the vast building, that he succeeded in locating the Dr P. P. Shah mentioned in the CBI officers' report as having Bala Chambhar under his care. Back and forth he had made his way through the endless labyrinth of long, white-tiled corridors, spittle splashed with red betelnut juice. A dozen times he was told by a dozen different, indifferent people ranging from the Resident Medical Officer down to ward boys that without Dr Shah's agreement there could be no question of his even seeing Bala Chambhar, let alone of finding out whether he had emerged from his coma.

But at last he found himself outside an office with a peon squatting next to its doorway and, beside the drooping green curtain that hung across it, a board saying *Dr P. P. Shah*.

'Doctor is inside?' he brusquely asked the peon, almost at exhaustion point now.

The man scrambled to his feet.

'No one may be seeing,' he muttered.

'I am a police officer. I am making inquiries. I need to see Dr Shah.'

'No one may be – '

Ghote jerked the green curtain aside and stepped through.

The reason, he found at once, why no one might be seeing Dr P. P. Shah was that the doctor was fast asleep in his not very clean white coat on a bare cot at the back of his little cabin.

Without hesitation Ghote marched across, took him by the shoulder and shook.

'What – What – '

'Dr Shah, I am a police officer. Inspector Ghote, Crime Branch. I am here to make inquiry about one Bala Chambhar admitted here suffering from poisoning, self-administered. And I am requiring your full assistance.'

Dr Shah heaved himself upright on the cot, blinked several times and scratched hard at his left armpit.

'What Bala Chambhar it is?' he said drowsily. 'I am having too many patients to know names and what-all.'

'He is a boy who was brought in here after attempting suicide only,' Ghote said. 'He was called as the culprit in one exam paper theft.'

'Ah. Ah, yes. Bed 52. Very, very interesting case.'

Dr Shah rubbed vigorously at his eyes, turned back to the cot, located his spectacles at the bed's head, and put them on.

'Yes, yes,' Ghote said, his spirits reviving as he saw the doctor taking more notice. 'A case Delhi itself is altogether interested in.'

'Delhi, Delhi. What am I caring about Delhi?' Dr Shah answered, heaving himself to his feet.

He went over to a basin in the corner and spat.

'No,' he said, 'case is interesting from medical point of view. It was I myself who was spotting unusual symptoms and sending specimens for analysis. And you are knowing result?'

Ghote, weary in body and mind, did not in the least care what the result of any medical analysis might be. But he had to keep on the good side of Dr Shah.

'Yes? What it is?' he asked.

'Somnomax Five,' Dr Shah answered triumphantly.

'Somnomax? What is that? There were five of them only?'

'No, no. Somnomax Five is one somnifacient.'

A little leap in Ghote's brain saved him from having to ask what the long word meant. 'Somnolent', was it not an equivalent of 'sleepy'?

'They are sleeping pills?' he said briskly. 'The boy, Bala Chambhar, was committing suicide by taking sleeping pills?'

'Yes, that is so,' Dr Shah replied, evidently a little put out that his diagnosis should have been so quickly caught up with by a layman. 'He had taken almost the fatal dose of this new American somnifacient. First case we have had in whole hospital.'

'Oh, too good,' Ghote said. 'Too good, Doctor. First-class work.'

From Dr Shah's complacent expression it seemed the praise had been enough. Ghote ventured on what he had come all the way to ask.

'And the boy? I may see? He is out of coma now you are knowing what is the poison?'

Dr Shah laughed.

'Out of coma? Not at all. No, I tell you, Inspector, it is a hundred-to-one against that the boy will ever come out of that state. A thousand-to-one even.'

Ghote felt depression sweep down.

'He is not even murmuring? Saying one or two words only?'

'No, no. Nothing at all of that sort. It is profound coma. Profound. Not too far from expiry itself.'

'But I may see?' he said with a sigh he could not suppress.

'If you are wishing. Why not?'

Dr Shah led him along to what proved to be the nearest ward and, marching rapidly down its long lines of close-packed white-painted iron bedsteads with patients sitting cross-legged on them or apathetically lying on top of their thin striped mattresses, he came at last to Bed No 52.

A white, or whitish coarse sheet with *K E M Hospital* in red several times stamped on it had been drawn up over the inert body. But at the bed's foot the boy's calves and feet protruded, the soles calloused from long going without shoe or chappal, the calves pitted with the marks of years of boils, signs of poor nutrition. While, above, the boy's face stared up sightless to the ceiling.

And there was nothing more to see. That was it. A body, just visibly and slowly breathing. Those feet. A face that had lost any expression and might have been almost any age from fifteen to forty.

Ghote stood for a moment or two more looking.

There was not the slightest movement other than the faint up and down motion of the grey-white sheet over the chest.

He turned to Dr Shah.

'Thank you for all your helps,' he said.

End of trail. Nothing for it now but to go home. Protima would quickly get him something to eat. Or . . . Ought he to get that business over first?

And afterwards state he wanted to eat whatever it was he wanted to eat and not what Protima insisted that he really wanted?

He wandered slowly through the maze of white-tiled, red-splashed corridors. But all too soon he came out to the pale brown, stony expanse of the compound where his vehicle stood waiting.

Then – he felt it as a sudden mercy – a thought struck him. Bala Chambhar had a home address. It was Chawl No 4, Dadasaheb Phalke Marg. Opposite somewhere called the Vishnu Shoe Clinic. The details had been in the CBI report. He had them by-hearted. Surely it would be worth going there to see if the boy had left any sort of clues.

It might take him all the rest of the afternoon to find the place. Perhaps even longer. There was a whole slum behind Dada Phalke Marg. Ved would be back at home before he reached there himself. So there would be no question of carrying out that beating today. A pity, but it could not be helped.

It did not take him long to find the Vishnu Shoe Clinic. It was a bright shop, with a red and yellow painted sign, devoted to the repair of shoes more complex than the simple chappals that pavement mochis dealt with as they squatted at street corners. A strong odour of new leather pervaded the whole pavement outside it. Chawl No 4 ought to be somewhere behind the shops on the other side.

But once he had squeezed through the narrow gap between two ornate and ancient buildings opposite – he had to turn sideways to negotiate it – his troubles began. He found himself in a bewildering jumble of close-packed wretched huts fabricated from pieces of galvanised iron, sheets of plastic and even the cut-up remains of huge painted film hoardings, with, rising up from them like storm-battered crags in a turbulent muddy sea, eight or nine tall, tottering chawls, accommodation built long ago for workers in the mills nearby. None, of course, with a number on it.

Working his way past mothers in thin, dirt-streaked saris crouching over little fires stirring at blackened cooking pots, past naked babies crawling feebly in the dust, past little girls in open-backed frocks and small boys wearing only holes-ripped half-pants, all mixed up with mange-marked dogs, scrawny pecking chickens and the occasional rootling hairy black pig, he asked, whenever he saw anyone likely to know, where Chawl No 4 might be.

At last a leering, bold-breasted chukla leaning at the open doorway of her hut told him where it was, despite his having hastily brushed aside her invitation. Now it was only a matter of discovering someone who happened to know on which floor was the room, out of the dozens on either side of the central corridors, where the Chambhar family lived.

He picked at last on a boy of nine or ten who, despite a much scabbed face, was possessed of a pair of brightly sharp eyes.

'Bachcha. Bala Chambhar? He is living here?'

The sharp eyes looked up at him.

'Policewalla, nai?'

Amazing how a boy like this could pick him out for what he was, despite his wearing shirt and pants like any one of hundreds of thousands of Bombayites.

'Ji haan, police,' he answered. 'But I am not making troubles.'

The boy considered briefly. Then spoke.

'Come.'

He led Ghote up three flights of rickety wooden stairs, greasy and dangerous with years of use. Here and there along the corridor at the top men were stretched out on the bare floor or on much frayed grass mats, stertorously asleep in the mustily humid air.

'Here,' the boy said, pointing to the door of one of the rooms. 'Chambhar Mrs inside only. Bala hospital. Dying soon.'

Ghote hoped that he was not hearing what might prove to be the truth. His best chance still was Bala recovering consciousness enough to say something indicating what the link was between the question-paper disappearing from Principal Bembalkar's chamber and copies being sold by Bala himself up and down Bombay. But he had an unpleasant feeling that his sharp little scabby-faced guide might know, somehow, more than he did, for all that it was scarcely an hour since he had seen with his own eyes Bala lying in a state of utter suspension, apparently neither going towards death nor coming slowly back to the living.

He knocked at the door the boy had indicated.

After a moment it was cautiously opened an inch or two. A woman in a white widow's sari with a seamed and suspicious face, peered out. Eye-catchingly evident was a scar-surrounded hole in her right nostril where once some pitiful nose-jewel had lodged before even that had had to be sold.

Ghote told her who he was.

With a chesty sigh she opened the door far enough to let him in.

The room he saw was so bare of possessions that it might have been awaiting some new tenant. Another thin white sari, with a carefully sewn patch all too visible in it, hung across the narrow barred window, perhaps as a curtain, perhaps to dry after washing. Otherwise the sole decoration on the long-ago painted green walls, here and there dark with hair-oil stains, was a crinkled oleograph of Dr Ambedkar, the great Untouchable leader, with at one corner of it the Buddha set against a plummy red background, gold-surrounded. Two charpoys, their cords frayed and sagging were the only items of furniture. On the high shelf along one wall stood a battered, much scratched can of kerosene, fuel for the single cooking ring on the floor, with beside it, making it by contrast look all the more wretched, a bright little plastic tub that had once contained sweet, saffron-flavoured shrikhand from one of the smart Monginis cake shops.

But nowhere was there any sign of the Oceanic College student who, according to the CBI report, had lived here. No books, no writing materials, nothing.

Ghote's spirits sagged. No, there was not going to be any clue here to the boy Bala. No nice middle-class notebook or diary scrawled with the names, addresses or even telephone numbers of dozens of friends. Friends in whom he might have confided, have laughingly told how he had been given that money-spinning advance question-paper.

Perhaps Bala had left home months and months ago? Slept where he could with friends or fellow students? Or perhaps it was just that such study books as he had once bought or borrowed had been sold.

'Your son, Bala,' he said carefully to the battered creature who had been watching him with poking suspiciousness as he had made his survey of her bare home, 'are you knowing who are his friends?'

'Hospital,' the old woman said, a gleam of cunning in her rheumy eyes. 'Taking his life, they are saying.'

'Well,' Ghote answered, trying for what comfort he could, much though he suspected the old woman's answer had been designed to give nothing away that might help a policewalla, 'We all of us in this world at times wonder whether we should pull on or be giving up.'

'They are saying he is one badmash,' the old woman went on with obstinate cunning. 'But he was a good son to me. He had promised a new sari from what he was making by selling that paper, whatever it was.'

Ghote sighed. He was going to learn nothing here. And, in fact, was it likely that an old woman like this would know Bala's college friends and possible accomplices? She had probably no idea what a question-paper really was. She would know nothing at all of exams or invigilation, of cheating and how it was all too often done. The chances that she was even able to read must be minimal.

What, if anything, would her bright but dishonest son have told her of his lucky reaching up to the status of college student. How much about it would she have been able to grasp? What dim notions must have passed through her mind, if he had said anything at all.

No way out of the adage here.

And nothing more in this bare room to give the least clue to that link between stolen question-paper and question-paper seller.

He turned to go, sullen despair welling up.

But then, at the very last moment, Bala's mother broke into what seemed to be a wail of genuine misery. But, despite the small upswelling of pity he suddenly felt for her, what she said gave him an unexpected spurt of hope.

'He was coming back from Lucky Copy Centre. He was going out once more with those paper-papers. Then, when he was coming home next, soon-soon he was falling asleep and not waking. Not waking. Not waking. Not ever waking.'

'But he may wake,' Ghote said, with a jab of remorse. 'I have seen one hour ago only at KEM Hospital, and he is alive still. He is alive. He may come back to you yet.'

With those words of hope, false hope he all too sharply feared, he left, clattering down the greasy wooden stairs fast as he could go. Now he had at least one more place to make inquiries. The Lucky Copy Centre.

9

The Lucky Copy Centre – Ghote had glimpsed its name as he had come up along Dadasaheb Phalke Marg – was only half a dozen shops down from the Vishnu Shoe Clinic. It would be the natural place for Bala Chambhar to get the stolen question-paper copied. Someone bound to be still there, even though darkness had now fallen, might know one of the boy's friends, or at least be able to describe them. So, Ghote thought, as he waited for a break in the jostling, swerving rush-hour traffic, this is really one good hope.

The place, when he had at last got across the road to it, hardly matched, however, its name and the big signboard he had noticed – *All Sorts of Petitions Notices Agreements Power of Attorneys Etc Is Undertaken.* Under a makeshift roof spanning a small gap between two buildings a single dented and paint-scarred copying machine was the sole service offered. Its operator, a man of late middle age with a round bald head and a pair of large-lensed pinkish-framed spectacles plastered across his face, was deeply absorbed in a newspaper spread across the top of its flimsy wooden counter.

Ghote placed himself in front of him.

The operator remained unmoved.

Ghote gave a rat-tat of a cough.

Still no response. The fellow was locked on to the Death Notices, a grubby-nailed finger slowly making its way down the column.

Leaning forward, Ghote seized the digit between his own finger and thumb and lifted it off the page.

Now the diligent reader did look up, peering apprehensively through his pinkish-framed spectacles.

'Police,' Ghote jabbed out. 'Now, you are knowing a youth from round here by the name of Bala Chambhar?'

The man considered, eyes blinking slowly behind the round lenses.

'I am' – he paused – 'knowing, yes.'

'Good. And Bala was coming here last Monday in the evening to have some work done?'

'Last' – pause – 'Monday . . .'

A longer pause. What on earth could he be hesitating over?

'Yes. Monday.'

Ghote pushed on, feeling at every moment more confident.

'Good, good. You were seeing what it was the boy was having copied, isn't it?'

'I was – ' another long-drawn pause – 'seeing.'

'It was a question-paper, no? A University of Bombay question-paper, Statistical Techniques?'

'It – might – Yes. Yes, it . . . was.'

Exasperation flamed up in Ghote.

'Why were you allowing?' he shouted. 'You must have been knowing this was one illegal document. Why were you letting that boy make copies by hundreds and hundreds?'

'Twenty . . . seven. Eight, one free.'

'All right, twenty-eight. But nevertheless why were you allowing?'

'I was – '

Deep consideration showed itself on the round face behind the pink-framed spectacles.

' . . . not.'

'Not what? Not what?'

Ghote jumped in before another impossible pause arrived.

'I was not,' the fellow repeated with maddening slowness, 'knowing this was one new paper. I was not . . . looking so closely. Sometimes students are wishing – '

And then the pause did come, the careful choice of the next word.

'To . . . examine old papers to see old questions.'

Now it was Ghote's turn to consider. Was the fellow lying? But what if he was? Copying that question-paper was not the greatest crime in the world. It might have been better, in fact, if he himself had not banged out that accusation with such ferocity. But the fellow was really too much.

He drew in a careful breath.

'Very well,' he said, 'I can understand you may have been a one hundred percent innocent party. Bala was saying nothing to you about that paper?'

Long pause.

'No.'

Ghote plunged quickly on.

'Well, was Bala with some friends when you were doing business?'

'He was with – '

Ghote waited, patting himself on the back for the patience he was showing. Who would it turn out to be? Would this fellow know the name? Was the tiny thread really going to lead onwards and onwards?

' . . . no one.'

'No one?' Ghote could not help firing back, bullet-like. 'You are saying he was with – '

He brought himself to a stop. Drew in another breath.

'Bala was here on his own?' he asked more quietly. 'You are sure? No friend hanging in background?'

'No.' Pause. 'No. No one. Not on Monday evening. Not – '

Another long, considering wait.

' . . . on Tuesday.'

Ghote's heart leapt.

'He was here again on Tuesday? Bala Chambhar was here on Tuesday? What time it was? What for was he here?'

'More – ' Pause. 'Copying.'

'Of that same paper? Was it? Was it?'

'Yes . . . He was coming . . . early. He had then more – '

'More money, yes?'

The fellow looked faintly aggrieved at his answer being anticipated in mid-flow. If his drawn-out words could possibly be described as flow.

'Yes, more . . . money. Fifty . . . extra copies.'

Calm, Ghote said to himself. Take it slowly, very, very slowly.

'What time was this on Tuesday?'

'As soon as . . . I . . . was opening. Eight o' . . . clock sharp.'

Ghote thought. This might well be significant. Apparently Bala was happily getting more copies of his stolen paper made at 8 a.m. on the day he had been admitted to hospital after taking those sleeping pills. So what had happened between those two events? When had the boy learnt the police were on his tracks and had decided abruptly to take the way out he had chosen? If it proved possible to trace him a little later than his eight o'clock visit here, he might yet find someone Bala had told about the link between Principal Bembalkar's chamber and the first sales of the paper. Whatever it was.

Then surely the cat would be free of the adage. He could file that report at last, and it would be an altogether better example of police work than the single sheet the CBI fellows had produced.

But tracing Bala from the time he had left the copy centre was not going to be easy.

He turned and looked at the road behind him under the bluey white light of the street lamps. Traffic was still hooting and pushing along, as at eight o'clock on last Tuesday morning it would have been doing in the opposite direction but with even more stink and vigour. So Bala would have been lost to the copy-shop operator's sight as soon as he had set off. And the pavement was, if anything, even more crowded and crammed than the roadway. People of all sorts were making their way up and down it, coolies with headloads of every variety, crates, an oil-drum, big bundles of heaven knows what, and businessmen, white-capped with clean white dhotis falling from fat stomachs, children dodging and running, secretaries and shop assistants in saris of every colour under the sun, and a beggar thrusting his way against the flow, dirty palm pushed out to anyone who looked as if they would produce a coin or two. That, too, would have been no different at eight o'clock last Tuesday, except that people would have been making their way to work instead of coming away from it.

No, no hope at all of tracing Bala's movements as he had left with his supply of newly copied question-papers. And where would he have gone? It was anybody's guess. To hang about, certainly, outside one of the colleges of Bombay University waiting to offer his advance information about those Statistical Techniques questions to any student willing to pay. But which college would he have chosen? Elphinston, of course. The trail had begun with a student from there. But, otherwise, no telling. No telling at all.

He felt the clustering sticks and thorny creepers of the adage once more unyielding around him.

But, damn it, he was not going to be defeated now, not when he had at last made one small advance.

He stood there on the crowded pavement and thought.

Yes, there was only one thing to do. He would have to go back to Oceanic College and get hold of any student who had been a particular friend of Bala's. The boy could not have been so secretive as never to give even a hint to some close pal about the wonderful money-spinning thing that had somehow come into his hands. But – he looked at his watch – no point in going out there again now. No one would be there, any more than they had been that first night.

So it was home.

And – the thought came rushing into his mind like water from a suddenly turned-on tap – was this the time to do what had to be done about Protima? But no sooner had he asked himself the question than he realised that Ved should be back by this hour. So the matter would not at all arise. It could, after all, wait. The right moment would come sooner or later. The main thing was that his mind was made up. Definitely.

Only would Ved perhaps have gone out again? To some friend?

For a long moment he hesitated where he was. But then, unable to think of any reason to do other than make his way homewards, he set off.

And found he was in luck. As soon as he tapped on the outer door he heard Ved's rushing footsteps coming towards him.

But why, he asked himself at once, had he thought of Ved being at home as good luck. Would good luck truly have been if Ved had been out, and if he could have dealt with Protima there and then?

She had cooked a meal that was supposed to be a favourite of his. And was.

So, after an evening of quiet domesticity, he was able to leave home next morning in good time to arrive at Oceanic College well before the 7.30 a.m. start of lectures.

Now, he thought, I must just only ask each and every student I am seeing, and sooner or later I would get hold of that good friend of Bala's. And then . . . Then, with just somewhat of luck, the secret of how the Statistical Techniques question-paper was spirited out of the Principal's chamber and into Bala's hands would be his. End of all that adage nonsense.

For a moment, standing just inside the tall iron gates of the college compound, he let his mind toy once again with that damn word. Adage? Addage? Which was it? And what, oh what, did it really mean?

But already, clustered round the cycle stand, a whole group of boys were putting their machines into the concrete racks under the supervision of the attendant, a noisy and opinionated fellow who, from his accent as he shouted commands, largely ignored and mostly contradictory, must be a South Indian.

Ah, he thought, just what I am wanting. Ten – fifteen possible witnesses, each to hand.

He hurried over.

But the first boy he drew aside promptly denied ever having known Bala.

'But you must be knowing all the boys in your year?' he said incredulously.

'Well, it is possible I am not knowing each and every – But, no. No, Bala was not at all in my year. Not at all.'

The boy turned away.

'Stop,' Ghote snapped.

His tone was enough to bring the young man to a quivering halt.

'What year is it you are?' Ghote demanded, trying hard at the same time to recollect how long Bala had been at the college. Someone had mentioned it. Had it been fat little Dean Potdar?

But it seemed the effort of trying to remember had taken something from the authority with which he had made his demand. The boy hesitated for an instant and then said with loud bravado 'I am first-year. Definitely first-year. Bala was second-year only.'

Ghote was almost certain the claim was a blatant lie. But, he decided, disproving it would entail altogether too many complications. And, besides, there were plenty of other witnesses there waiting.

It proved, however, that this encounter with the liar had been overheard by all the students at the cycle stand. Some had simply walked hurriedly away, and each of the others he detained immediately claimed also to be a first-year and not to have known Bala.

For a moment Ghote wondered why they were so reluctant.

But it was easy enough to understand. Bala had got himself mixed up with the police. The only sure way to avoid getting caught up in the same net was to deny and deny. And denying and denying each of his potential witnesses was.

He had been vaguely aware all the time that other students were arriving, mostly girls in bright saris or trousered salwar-kameez, and had been hurrying into the building behind him. He glanced at his watch now. Already twenty-eight minutes past seven. Had he missed all his chances? Were the spines and whippy lengths of bamboo of the adage – he found he was sure now it was some sort of monkey trap – flicking across behind him even more thickly?

But then a last boy on a bicycle came swerving in through the gate and headed at speed for the cycle stand. Ghote recognised him. He was the young shaven but turban-wearing, rebellious Sikh who had been one of the leaders of the night morcha.

The boy brought his cycle to a sideways-tilting halt, swung a leg over the saddle and thrust the machine towards the attendant.

Ghote stepped up to him and laid a hand on his arm.

'I am wanting one word.'

The young Sikh looked at him, evidently recognising him from that night encounter. Sparking rebellion gathered in every limb of his body.

'It is our right to take out any procession we are wishing,' he said, his voice rising. 'What for are you damned policewallas interfering and interfering?'

'I am not at all interfering,' Ghote answered, secretly delighted that the boy had retorted with such fire since just one conciliatory word should make him pliable as wax from a bees' nest. 'Take out as many morchas as you are liking, by night or by day.'

And it seemed to work. The boy looked almost comically astonished.

'What is your good name?' Ghote asked, following up this success with all the friendliness he could muster.

'It is Mohinder Singh Mann,' the boy replied. 'But what it is you are wanting?'

Ghote smiled.

'Just only to find out two-three little things,' he said. 'You are knowing Bala Chambhar, isn't it?'

'Yes. Yes, I am knowing.'

But a note of caution had at once crept in. Plain to be heard.

'Were you seeing Bala last Tuesday?' Ghote asked quickly. 'I am trying to learn where he was in the time before the poor fellow was taking those pills that were almost causing him to expire.'

'Pills?'

Mohinder gave him a quick look he found hard to interpret.

'Yes,' Ghote said, 'were you not knowing that it was with sleeping pills that Bala was attempting his suicide?'

'No, no. It is news to me only,' the boy answered, his voice becoming vaguer and more distant with every word.

'Well, yes. That much I am ascertaining at KEM Hospital yesterday. But swallowing many, many pills or throwing oneself in front of oncoming train or into some well, it is all the same if one is determined to end one's life. No, what I am interested to find out is who Bala was seeing, who he was talking with, in those hours before he made up his mind to do that thing.'

He saw Mohinder stiffening in front of his eyes.

'Then, Inspector, I am not at all able to help. I was not seeing Bala that day, or for many days before. Not to be talking with.'

'I see. But are you knowing anybody who was? Who were his special friends in the college?'

Mohinder shrugged.

'I do not know, Inspector. I think he did not have too many friends. You know what it is with those harijan boys. You try to be nice to them but it is not easy to become fast friends when they are having such different lives.'

'Yes, all right. But can you think of one single boy or girl he was more friendly with than with others?'

'No. No, Inspector. I cannot. And I must go now. I must not be late for class.'

Ghote put a detaining hand on the boy's arm again and smiled.

'Oh, come,' he said, 'I am betting you have done many worse things than be two – three minutes late.'

'Yes. No. No, I must go.'

And the boy pulled his arm from Ghote's grasp and set off at a run towards the blank concrete-faced college building.

Ghote stood where he was, experiencing a vague sense of puzzlement. Something was not as it ought to be. Or as he had thought it was.

But he could not get at it.

He gave a shrug and turned towards the gate, with the half-formed idea in his mind that the best he could do now was to go over to the Paris Hotel tea shop and hope to find a few students idling there as there had been the day before.

Then just as he set off – the feeling of puzzlement dragged at him still – a loud voice spoke almost in his ear.

'Oah, that Mohinder Singh Mann is one damn bloody liar. Yes, I am saying it. Krishna Iyer, MA Madras, reduced to cycle-stand attendant.'

Ghote turned, taking his first good look at the man.

He was a big fellow, somehow of a slobbering build, all the more apparent since he wore only a bright, multi-coloured lungi wrapped round his waist and falling to somewhere near his ankles. His face, which was oval and fresh-looking as an egg, was marked by the single vertical thick white-painted line that indicated mastery of one of the sacred Vedas.

'What it is you are saying?' he asked him, more sharply than he had meant.

Krishna Iyer, MA Madras, grinned with wobbly unease.

'Oah, Inspector, I am not telling one word of untruth. I am always speaking truth, exact and complete. Oah yes. And I am saying that Mohinder Singh Mann is one bloody liar.'

'Very well, what was he lying about?'

'Bala Chambhar he is knowing very well. Student leader he may be and

Bala Chambhar worst boy in whole damn college, but they are heads together often and always.'

'Are they? But why are you telling me this?'

'Oah, Inspector, truth must prevail. That I am saying and stating. Truth must prevail. Never will I hesitate to say same.'

Ghote looked at him again.

'But I am thinking,' he said, the sight abruptly sharp in his mind of the Sikh boy carelessly shoving his bicycle towards the attendant, 'you would not be so keen for truth to prevail if it was someone else than Mohinder Singh Mann you were calling as a liar.'

'Oah, yes, Inspector. Too bloody right. That fellow is treating Krishna Iyer, MA Madras, as if he was a coolie only, fourth–fifth class.'

'So perhaps Mohinder is not so much of a liar?'

'No, no, Inspector. Truth must prevail. Mohinder Singh Mann was telling most gigantic whopper when he was saying he was not at all knowing Bala Chambhar.'

'Well, I believe you then.'

Ghote turned away, wondering whether he was in fact right to believe the slobbery South Indian, who after all seemed to be possibly a little mad, or more than a little. On the other hand, though, he might be no more than somewhat eccentric, and with graduate unemployment what it was it was no shame to him that, if he was indeed an MA, he was working as a cycle-stand attendant.

'Oah, Inspector, in one hour in canteen. Always.'

For a moment Ghote wondered how the cycle-stand attendant could know that. But then he thought how in a place like this, or anywhere really in talkative Bombay, everybody was apt to know everything about everybody. The fellow's loudly voiced hint reverberated after him, too, as he made his way towards the Paris Hotel. Was he merely attempting to gain revenge on Mohinder Singh Mann? Or was he, for all his oddity, really a believer that 'truth must prevail' in every circumstance?

Well, yes, he thought, whichever way it is, I suppose I had better go to the canteen in an hour and tackle that young man. After all, that is almost the only line I have.

Bembalkar's resignation. Demands, if what he had gathered had been going on behind the Principal's door was right, Dr Bembalkar had been prevented from yielding to only with a prolonged barrage of arguments.

But what to do by way of finding out if all that was part and parcel of the business? Nothing, until he had some hard facts about what had actually happened. And those, as the CBI wallas had quickly realised, were not going to come from that boy lying in a coma in the KEM Hospital.

Still, they might, just might, come from a few determined words with young Mohinder Singh Mann.

The hour before classes broke was not yet up. But as soon as he reached the gates again he marched into the building. A painted arrow on the far wall, for all that it was almost smothered by vaguely political messages in Marathi and English scrawled all over the once-white surface, directed him to the student canteen.

It turned out to be a depressing, low-ceilinged room crammed with too many grey plastic-topped tables and cooled by too few ceiling fans. At the far end a tea-urn stood on a counter, also in grey plastic, with ranged behind it a stack of crates containing Limca and Fanta bottles, pale greenish yellow or full orange. Otherwise the place was empty.

He looked at his watch.

As he flopped down at a table in a corner, glad to rest after his long walk in the sun, he found his thoughts sliding away. To his wife.

What was it going to be best to use for what he had to do? A chappal off one of his feet? No, too much of a childish thing. A whip then? A good whipping? No, no. Altogether too much of cruel. What was wanted was simply to show Protima, definitely, who was boss. So some sort of a cane? Like the one his father had had as a schoolmaster, and had not hesitated to use? Or a belt? That was what the gup-shup at Headquarters usually mentioned. A good leather belt.

Only he did not, as it happened, possess such a thing.

He sighed.

It was difficult. Difficult. But action had to be taken, definitely.

From outside there came a sudden loud splat of clattering feet. First classes over. Mohinder Singh Mann would be here at any moment.

Good. Something really to get down to. Instead of . . .

Mohinder did not come with the first rush of students, racing across to the counter and calling clamorously for service. But, to Ghote's relief, the young Sikh was not far behind. He watched him as he went to the crush at the counter and eventually came away with two bottles of Fanta.

10

The Paris Hotel provided Ghote with no new line to pursue. There was no one at all at its tables. The proprietor, the moment he had stepped inside, greeted him with even more eagerness than he had welcomed the blustering Punjabi security officer, Amar Nath with.

'Inspector, Inspector. Very nice to see. You are liking Paris Hotel very much, yes? You are coming here each and every day? Inspector, you will never have to pay one paisa. It is an honour to have such a burra sahib to eat my food. Boy! One double egg omelet for the inspector. Big eggs, big eggs. The biggest.'

'No,' Ghote said in an explosion of rejection, fuelled not a little by the horrible odour everywhere of over-boiled tea. 'No, I was just only looking in. I must go. I must go. Appointment.'

He retreated, at once furious with himself for reacting so violently to that gush of ridiculous flattery. But perhaps, he thought, he had been still somehow put off-balance by something in his encounter with Mohinder Singh Mann, or by the cycle-stand attendant's comments afterwards.

However, sorting that out must wait till the Sikh boy got to the canteen.

To pass the time till then he made his way round the whole stretch of Oceanic College's railings-guarded compound. It was, he soon realised, absurd to walk so far in the already strongly sullen heat. But once begun there was nothing else for it but to go on.

There must be a lot of money invested in the college, he thought idly as he tramped along, if it could occupy so much land. Would it be a profitable investment? Well, if someone like Mrs Rajwani, wife of Rajwani Enterprises, was at the head of the trustees, the concern was almost certainly worth her time. So, was it important that its Principal should be a mild academic, easily made to do whatsoever the trustees wanted? Or to overlook whatsoever they wanted overlooked?

And did this have any bearing on the theft of the question-paper? It might do. It might. After all, demands now had been made for Principal

Getting to his feet, he set off on a path that would cross the boy's. Other students, precariously holding cups of tea or clutching handfuls of cold-drink bottles, were hurrying to any vacant table, shouting to friends, exchanging insults, fooling. In the turmoil he momentarily lost sight of his quarry.

Then he saw him. He had found a place at a table. But there waiting was green-blooming, wind-swayed Sarita Karatkar, last seen when he had cunningly thwarted her by implying in front of her fellow night marchers that she had been helping the police, fearful treason.

He cursed. He had seen himself getting Mohinder on his own and observing his least reaction as he banged at him an accusation of lying about his friendship with Bala Chambhar. But, with that sparky creature there, it might not be so easy to get the boy away on his own.

He strode across, however.

'Mohinder Singh Mann,' he said, grimly formal. 'I am wanting one word. In private.'

'It is Inspector Ghote,' Sarita Karatkar bounced in, mischief at once twinkling in her eyes.

'Yes, yes,' he answered, somehow pleased she did not seem to bear him a grudge. 'Good morning, Miss Karatkar.'

He turned again to the Sikh.

'Now,' he said, 'kindly come with me.'

But again it was the girl who answered.

'Whatever do you want with Mohinder, Inspector? You're not going to drag him off in handcuffs for leading our morcha?'

'No, no. Already I have told, he can take out as many morchas as he is wanting. No, it is something altogether different I am wishing to talk.'

'Then talk away, Inspector. There's nothing about Mohinder I don't know.'

She turned to the boy then.

'Or is there?' she asked, sparkling with innocent enjoyment. 'What have you been hiding in the Student Union office, Mohinderji? Was it some dirty books that whoever it was who tried to break in there last week was wanting? Or are you living on immoral earnings only? Or – I know – you have outraged the modesty of one–two thousand women. Confess, confess.'

The tall young Sikh grinned at her.

'Oh, if it was just only dirty books that thief, whoever he was, wanted he would be welcome to take and to take,' he said. 'But what it was, if you are asking me, is documents about how we are planning to get something of justice in this college.'

And Ghote found that, despite what might be illegal activities the young Sikh and his friends were planning, there had been such a shining light of idealism in what he had said that he could not but look on him favourably. If India still produced young people as well-intentioned and bubbling with energy as Mohinder, and for the matter of that as impudent Sarita, then perhaps the student world was not in such a bad state as he had come to believe.

He realised too, that, since he would not in fact be taking the boy away for any offence, he had better reconcile himself to putting his question about Bala Chambhar with Sarita sitting there and with the noise of all the other students – a group at one table were blowing tunes across the tops of their partly empty Limca bottles – all around.

'Very well,' he said. 'Mohinder, I have to ask just only one thing. Why did you lie to me about how well you were knowing Bala Chambhar?'

But yet again Sarita Karatkar bounced cheerfully in.

'Oh, Mohinderji, were you trying to lie to Inspector Ghote? You should know he is not at all a person you can deceive. Very, very clever man.'

Mohinder pulled a face.

'I'm sorry, Inspector,' he said. 'I really should have known better.'

'You should have been better,' Sarita said. 'Telling lies. Oh, Mohinder.'

'Yes, well, I do try not to tell more lies than I have to,' the boy conceded. 'But, to tell you the truth – '

'Shabash, shabash,' Sarita broke in. 'Holy truth at last.'

'To tell you the truth, Inspector,' Mohinder went on, 'I had from the moment I was hearing that Bala had tried to take his life, a feeling of uneasy. And because I didn't want too much to look that feeling in the full face I pretended I knew Bala less well than I did.'

Ghote remained silent. He was conscious that he had just learnt something. Something perhaps well worth learning.

'Well, Inspector, aren't you going to slap this boy about just a little?' Sarita demanded. 'Such a lying riff-raff as he is.'

'No,' Ghote answered slowly. 'No, I shall have to leave you now.'

He got up and went quickly out of the noisy, crowded room – 'Pass the cigarette, pass the cigarette,' a boy shouted as he went by – because there were things he had to think about. What Mohinder Singh Mann had said had been just the little push needed to send a whole train of incidents and observations sliding and rattling into place.

What it is, he said to himself, crystallising it, is that Bala Chambhar was not at all trying to commit suicide. Someone has attempted to murder him.

11

The evidence, Ghote thought, had really mounted and mounted from the very start of his investigation. First there had been what Sarita Karatkar had actually said to him as they had marched along side by side during that night morcha. She had said Bala Chambhar did not seem to her to be someone who would take his own life. At the time, he had put that down to the simple optimism of youth. A girl as full of young hope as Sarita would find it hard to imagine someone her own age being driven to suicide.

Then, at the hospital, he had been told directly that Bala had attempted suicide by taking Somnomax Five tablets, and Dr Shah had even added that these were a new 'somnifacient' from America. But, proud of himself at that moment for guessing what the medical term meant, he had altogether overlooked the fact that it was extremely unlikely that a poverty-stricken boy like Bala could have got hold of an expensive, American-imported prescription.

Why, something he had said to young Mohinder this very morning had even set the matter out. If anyone was determined to take their own life, he had said, it did not much matter whether they swallowed pills, hurled themselves in front of a train or threw themselves into a well. But he had been wrong. The choice of method did not matter looked at in the light of the final result, perhaps. But, looked at in the light of what choice was available to a particular person contemplating suicide, it certainly did matter. An unmarried girl out in some deep mofussil area who had found herself pregnant would throw herself into the village well. A Bombayite from the weaker sections, as they were called, would choose a train, if he could not find a rope and a place high enough to hang it. Only someone of the well-off classes would use expensive American sleeping pills or blow out his brains with a sporting gun.

Nor had that been all. Somehow in that bare little room in Chawl No 4 off Dadasaheb Phalke Marg he had looked at the smart shrikhand tub from a Monginis cake shop up on the shelf next to the battered kerosene tin, and had thought only of how shabby it made the tin look. It had never occurred to him to wonder how a bright new tub of best quality shrikhand had arrived in the wretched little room.

But he knew now. He knew now all right.

That tub had been sent to Bala Chambhar, or put somehow in his way, because – surely, surely the shrikhand in it had been mixed with crushed-up tablets of Somnomax Five. Only, whoever had put them in had, by chance, not used quite enough. So Bala Chambhar had not yet died, but instead was lying in that coma.

Nevertheless murder had been attempted. The whole business out here at Oceanic College looked altogether different now. He must report at once to the Additional Commissioner.

But what was he to report? Coming down to it, no more than a single train of thought.

For a moment he imagined himself standing in front of the Additional Commissioner's desk with no more to tell him than what had just gone through his head. A whisper of suspicion. No, the Additional Commissioner would hardly give him kudos for that.

But if he could get some evidence . . . Just only one decent shred of same.

Wait. Yes, the tub of shrikhand. If that had crushed Somnomax Five mixed in, then chemical analysis of the last traces of the sweet stuff in the tub might well reveal it. That would be proof enough that Bala Chambhar's state of coma was not the result of attempted suicide. No one with tablets to swallow would go to the lengths of crushing them into a sweetmeat.

For a moment he contemplated hurrying down to Dadasaheb Phalke Marg and Chawl No 4 again. But the mere time the expedition would take daunted him. No, there was a better and quicker way. The local police station.

He took the stairs up to the first floor and Principal Bembalkar's office almost at a run. Mrs Cooper was, of course, at her desk, guardian rakshas. But a rakshas he had found earlier could be a helpful beast, almost ready to lick his hand with her fiery tongue.

And certainly quite ready to put the telephone at his disposal. Nor was the Station House Officer at Dadar Police Station any less helpful, a rare local officer who did not resent a Crime Branch colleague. Yes, he would send someone to Chawl No 4 off Dadasaheb Phalke Marg, opposite the Vishnu Shoe Clinic, and impound one tub of shrikhand, Monginis cake shops, and hold same for Inspector Ghote. It would be one only pleasure.

Yet, replacing the telephone receiver, he once more experienced plummeting depression. Even with the evidence of the doctored shrikhand secured, how could he link up the stolen question-paper to the poisoned boy? Bala Chambhar could not, unless at last he was to recover, tell how he had come by that tub. Any more than he could tell how he had received the question-paper he could not himself have taken from Principal Bembalkar's chamber. But it was to prevent him saying this – he was certain of it in his own mind – that the poison had been put in Bala's way. The poison that had so nearly succeeded in ending his life.

Who had put it there? If, standing at attention in front of the Additional Commissioner, he could perhaps produce a likely name, with good reasons why the person should have needed to silence Bala, then what he had to say would be listened to with somewhat of respect.

But who had done that? Who? No name at all sprang to mind. It could have been anybody almost. Anybody in the whole of the college here.

Or perhaps not everyone in the college. To begin with whoever it was must be someone who, unlike Bala, could afford Somnomax Five. All right, there might be dozens of boys or girls with parents well-off enough. But why, when you came down to it, would a well-off student want to steal that question-paper and make money from it. Yes, there might be someone in the BCom course worried about passing the Statistical Techniques exam and they might have daringly entered the Principal's office. But they would not have removed the question-paper. It would have been enough for them to have seen what the questions were.

So why would someone not only have taken the paper but have contrived to hand it to Bala in the knowledge that he would make what money he could by distributing it? It was very likely, after all, that sooner or later it would have come out that copies had been widely sold. The exam would be annulled. No gain would come to anybody. The trick would have worked only because it was certain that Bala would be careful not to tell any of his prospective clients that other copies existed.

Why then, why had the thief passed the question-paper on to Bala?

In a moment he thought he had the answer. The whole business, surely, had been designed with one object. To get rid of Principal Bembalkar. Because that was what had been achieved, or would have been achieved except that influential Mrs Rajwani wanted to keep Dr Bembalkar in his seat and had spent most of a morning persuading him not to give in to calls for his resignation. And how beaten down he had looked after that long session. Scarcely capable of answering the simplest question.

Well then, who would benefit if Principal Bembalkar resigned? Easy answer. Whoever thought themselves most likely to step into his shoes. A sudden vision of fat little Dean Potdar presented itself in his mind. Yes, surely the man most likely to succeed the Principal of a college must be its Dean. And even someone as low in the college hierarchy as securitywalla Amar Nath had hinted that Dean Potdar of the many daughters despised the Principal. So who more likely to want his chair?

But evidence. More than supposition would be needed before he could go to the Additional Commissioner, even with a good suspect in mind. Where to get some evidence? Anything that would confirm his suspicions.

Yet surely he had at least one good hostile witness ready to hand. If there were things to be learnt about the man who wanted to step into Principal Bembalkar's shoes, then the person who so plainly had a soft corner for the Principal would surely supply them.

He turned back to Mrs Cooper.

Hardly pausing to calculate whether it was wise to put his theory to anyone other than the Additional Commissioner, he found himself beginning to pour it out to the fierce guardian of Principal Bembalkar's peace. It looked certain now, he said, that Bala Chambhar had not tried to kill himself but was the victim of a murder attempt that had come within an inch of succeeding.

Mrs Cooper jerked back in astonishment.

'Yes, yes,' he went rapidly on. 'And, you are knowing, that attempt was made for just only one purpose. To prevent Bala saying how the stolen question-paper was coming into his possession. You see, I am believing the paper was taken for no other reason than to force Principal Bembalkar to resign.'

Mrs Cooper took a moment or two to absorb this. Then she nodded slowly in agreement.

'Yes, Inspector,' she said. 'Some drama is being staged behind the curtain. That I can tell you.'

'That only?'

He gave her a knowing look, as much as to say he was sure she could say more if she would.

Mrs Cooper smiled down into her typewriter.

'Well, mind, I don't know everything,' she said.

'No. But there are some things a lady in your seat cannot help knowing. When you are in a position of trust . . .'

The rakshas positively simpered now.

'Well,' she said, 'it is certainly true there have been demands for Principalji to step down. And the scandal of that question-paper being taken – how could anyone do such a thing to Dr Bembalkar? – has made things altogether worse. The University itself even is sending LIC here tomorrow.'

Ghote found himself then in a minor dilemma. He did not know what 'LIC' stood for. But if he stopped the flow of information, hardly as yet hardly much more than a trickle, would it start again and reach the point he hoped it would get to?

'Please,' he burst out, before he had come to any decision, 'what is LIC?'

Luckily the opportunity to give instruction seemed to outweigh for once the chance of darting out a rebuke.

'LIC is Local Inquiry Committee,' Mrs Cooper said, with a proud lift of her bosom under her red blouse. 'It is appointed by the University when there is reason to believe affairs at any one college are not as they should be.'

She blushed suddenly then.

'Not that there is truly anything to sorrow about here,' she said quickly. 'We are victim of nasty rumours. That is all. Mrs Rajwani is very very disgusted at what is being done.'

'Yes, yes,' Ghote chimed in, relieved that the Anglo-Indian seemed as willing as ever to talk. 'It seems to be altogether a bad business. But, tell me, if attempt is being made to force Principalji to quit, who can be behind it? Who would step into his seat?'

'Oh, Inspector,' Mrs Cooper said, looking modestly down again, 'it is not for me to name names.'

Ghote thought he knew how to deal with that sort of reluctance.

'You are right not to indulge in gossip and rumour,' he said. 'Hundred percent correct behaviour.'

His ploy worked.

'But all the same, Inspector, when it is official police inquiry . . .'

'Yes?'

'Well, they could always bring in some person from outside . . .'

'But . . . ?'

'But I am thinking Mrs Rajwani would prefer angel she is knowing.'

'Ah, yes.' Ghote pounced. 'Let me say to you then just only one name. Dean Potdar.'

'Oh, no, no, no, Inspector. Dean Potdar is altogether out of question as successor to Principalji. You see, he is already age-barred.'

'Yes,' Ghote agreed, reluctant still to see such an obvious candidate, however getting on in age, struck out. 'But surely officers everywhere who are age-barred have been known, with somewhat of influence, to gain promotions.'

'Oh, that is true, yes. It is often happening. But, you see, with Dean Potdar it is a very, very different matter. If he was to go up to Principal his application would have to go to University itself. Authorisation must be granted. So there it would come to light that he is already past statutory age.'

'You are certain?'

'Oh, yes, yes.'

Mrs Cooper once more drew herself up with modest pride.

'You see,' she said, 'there has been question of him taking Principalji's seat before. It was the first time that Dr Bembalkar was wishing to devote himself altogether to writing his book. Mrs Rajwani even was agreeing to it then. And Dean Potdar had convinced her he would not – well, she was accepting him. Letters were passing through my hands. And in them it came out. No possibility to do it. So Mrs Rajwani was having one word with Dr Bembalkar himself, and no more was heard of matter.'

Ghote thought briefly that Mrs Rajwani's 'one word' must have been multiplied by several thousand when she had persuaded poor Principal Bembalkar that he could not retire to devote himself to *Hamlet*. But he had no time for such idle speculation. A thought more to the point had come to him. If Dean Potdar was really not a possible candidate for the Principal's seat, and it truly seemed that he was not, then the fat little malicious fellow was certainly a candidate for something else.

If he himself could keep up his act as a totally stupid police officer, then Dean Potdar, happily convinced he was all the time running rings round him, would be a first-class choice as informant. Far better than Mrs Cooper, willing only to defend her soft corner.

'Madam,' he said hastily as soon as this thought was fully formed in his mind, 'kindly excuse me now. I have important appointment.'

He hurried out, raced along the balcony outside to Dean Potdar's office, barged in, hastily asked the Dean's placidly knitting secretary if he was disengaged and, almost before he knew what he was doing, found himself, breathing a little rapidly, once more facing the tubby little academic.

'Well, Inspector, what brings you here in such a hurry? You have found how that question-paper was stolen from poor Bembalkar? You want to recount your triumph?'

'No, sir, no. Very regret I have no such good news. I am here only because you were so much of helpful before, and I am thinking you could be very-very helpful again.'

He hoped he had managed to set himself up once more as the half-educated police officer needing guidance from this academic master-mind.

It seemed he had. Dean Potdar's eyes twinkled merrily behind the pince-nez half-way down his podgy little nose.

'We must all do what we can to aid and assist our gallant police force,' he said. 'Sit, sit, and tell me your trouble, Inspector.'

Ghote perched himself on the edge of the same chair he had pulled out before from the row drawn up in front of the Dean's desk. He put a heavy frown on to his face.

'Well, sir,' he said. 'It is like this only. You see, from informations we are having it is now looking like as if that young fellow Bala Chambhar by name was not at all committing suicide.'

Dean Potdar looked as surprised by this as Mrs Cooper had done a few minutes earlier. Ghote, however, had little difficulty in deciding the air of astonishment was exaggerated for the benefit of this idiot police officer.

'Yes, sir,' he went on. 'Such is seeming to be the case. We are believing now that someone was giving the boy poison only. They were not wanting him to be saying that they had handed to him that question-paper they themselves had taken from the Principal's chamber with their own hands.'

'With their own hands, Inspector? Remarkable. Truly remarkable.'

'Yes, sir, it is one only diabolical plot.'

'I should say it is, Inspector. A diabolical plot. You put it very well.'

Ghote contrived to produce a smirking sort of smile.

'Oh, sir,' he said, 'there is more even to that plot.'

'More, Inspector? You astonish me.'

Ghote gravely wagged his head.

'Sir, do you know what it is we are thinking?' he said.

'Inspector, I cannot guess. You police fellows are so clever. Diabolically clever, if I may put it that way.'

Ghote produced the same smirk, a little disappointed that he could find no variant of it.

'Sir, it is like this,' he went on. 'We are asking what would be the object of this person unknown in handing that question-paper to a harijan student always in need of money. And this is what we are thinking. Sir, someone is plotting and planning to force Principal Bembalkar to resign.'

'You don't say so, Inspector? Plotting? And planning? That is altogether monstrous.'

'Yes, sir, yes. But this is why I am requesting and requiring your assistance, if you are able to give it. Sir, we are believing this person who is wanting Principal Bembalkar to quit his seat is seeking to take same.'

'To take same? Inspector, I think you have hit on the very motive. The very motive for – what did you call it? – that diabolical plot.'

'Yes, sir. Very-very diabolical.'

Was he overdoing it? But the Dean seemed to be sitting there enjoying himself to the full. So keep going.

'Now, sir, you must be knowing that a college like this is altogether difficult for me. I am not at all knowing what is making tick academic gentlemen in any way whatsoever.'

'Oh come, Inspector. I'm sure your native intelligence will help you out.'

Ghote sadly shook his head. Should he risk letting his mouth hang open? Perhaps not.

'Oh, no, sir. It has not at all helped out. I am floating in very-very deep seas, sir.'

'Well, my dear chap, if I can in any way help?'

'Oh, please, sir. That is what I was hoping to one hundred and one percent.'

'Very well then, Inspector, tell me what you want to know? Or can I guess? You want to know who would step into Principal Bembalkar's shoes were he to leave his post in disgrace. Is that it?'

'Sir, you have hit screw on head only.'

'Yes, well . . .'

Little Dean Potdar hesitated. Or appeared to hesitate.

'You know, Inspector,' he went on, 'you are putting me in a very awkward position. What you are doing, you see, is asking me to – to peach, I think is the word, on one or more of my colleagues.'

'Please, sir, what is peach?'

That was an easy one.

'Peach? Peach? Yes, perhaps an unusual English word. Slang, you know. Picked it up in my miscellaneous reading. It means, I believe, to tell tales on. To tell-tale against, perhaps you would say.'

'Oh, yes, sir. To tell-tale against. That is cent percent correct.'

Ghote let a silence fall. He had no doubt now that the Dean was going to produce the names of anyone in the college likely to succeed the Principal. No point in risking spoiling the game by fishing for the names more than necessary.

He did not have long to wait.

'However, Inspector, it is my duty. As you have indicated. And duty must be done, however unpleasant. So . . .'

'Yes, sir.'

He had no difficulty in assuming a properly puppy-dog look now. He was eager enough to hear the names, after all.

'Well, Inspector, I suppose, if pressed, I would have to say that the succession lies between three people.'

'Three, sir?'

'Yes, three. Do you want to make notes, Inspector?'

'Oh, yes, sir. Yes. Most important to keep one only accurate record.'

He fished out notebook and pencil. And remembered, just in time, to give the end of the pencil a good heavy lick.

'Ready, Inspector?'

'Yes, sir. Ready, steady, go.'

'Good. Then Number One: Dr Dinanath Kapur, or Professor Kapur, as he insists on calling himself. Lecturer in Astrology.'

The Dean gave a heavy sigh. And Ghote himself restrained only with difficulty a similar reaction. He still felt that a college of Bombay University, modern, up-to-date Bombay, even one as remote as Oceanic College, should not have such a lecturer on its staff.

But he dipped his head down and wrote busily in his notebook.

' . . . in astrology,' he murmured. 'Yes, sir, and Number Two?'

'Number two, Inspector. Dr Mrs Lakshmi Gulabchand, Head of the English Department.'

Ghote allowed himself to look up with a startled expression.

'Sir, you are saying that a lady only may be responsible for – ' he checked himself. 'For this diabolical plot, sir?'

Dean Potdar sighed. Very heavily.

'Inspector, I have to tell you that the female of the species is sometimes more deadly than the male.'

'Sorry, sir?'

'Women have been known to commit murder, Inspector.'

'Oh, yes, sir. Yes. I am seeing what you are meaning. Yes, that is altogether true. Two hundred percent.'

'So, do you want to hear the third name I have for you, Inspector?'

'Oh, yes, please, sir. That is being most helpful.'

'Then it is this. Dean N.N. Potdar.'

He very nearly caught Ghote out. Only a sudden almost choking effort kept back some such give-away reaction as 'But you are too old, the University has already rejected you'. Playing this game was not as easy as he had fallen into believing. He must remember that the man he was milking was no simpleton.

If the cat was slipping and sliding out of that adage – was it a contrivance of sharp kika thorn branches? – it was clear that at any moment new twisty lengths of the stuff could wrap themselves round him.

He quickly took advantage of the choking fit that had saved him, extending it till the blood rushed up into his face.

'Sir,' he said at last. 'Is it that you are saying that you yourself were murdering the boy Bala Chambhar?'

'Murdering, Inspector? But who has said that the boy has been murdered?'

'Oh, sir, sorry. Very-very sorry. I must be saying attempted murder. Sir, is it that you were committing one attempted murder?'

Dean Potdar's twinkling eyes glinted yet more brightly.

'Well, what do you think, Inspector?'

He took his time in answering. As a stupid police officer surely would have done too.

'Sir, it was never occurring to me that a gentleman such as yourself . . .'

'Well, it should have done, Inspector, should it not? However, as it happens, though I suppose from my position in the college, if by nothing else, I might be seen as a successor to poor Bembalkar, I am rather too aged to be able to accept the post.'

'Oh, I see, sir. Jolly good. I mean, not at all good that you are aged, sir but – but – '

'Yes, well, Inspector, perhaps we had better not pursue that line.'

'No, sir. No. But, please, sir, you are certain there are only three – no, two. Just only two people in the college who might succeed to Principal Bembalkar?'

Dean Potdar considered.

'Yes, Inspector, I think I can acquit each one of my other colleagues of the crime of wanting to step into Bembalkar's shoes. Or if not of wanting to, since ambition lurks in the most unlikely places, of having any real chance of so doing.'

Ghote pretended for a little to be working out what that had meant.

If Dean Potdar was right, he thought quietly to himself – and he had little doubt that had there been any other serious contender for the Principal's post the Dean would not have hesitated to put their name forward – then his task was less difficult than it might have been. He had only two suspects to try to find some good evidence against before he could go to the Additional Commissioner. And, he thought, there might well be some hard evidence to be got. Bala Chambhar had been reduced to his state of coma by Somnomax Five tablets. And Somnomax Five was not the sort of sleeping pill that would be found in very many Bombay homes. So it was possible that either Professor Kapur, Lecturer in Astrology, or Mrs Lakshmi Gulabchand, Head of English, might be found still to be in possession of a supply. Or there might be evidence – an empty packet, a torn scrap of a container – that they had had such a drug.

His task was clear before him.

12

Before Ghote left the Dean's office, however, he received a parting shot from the malicious little man.

He had got to his feet, mumbling thanks as incoherent as he could make them. If he could get the home addresses of his two suspects from the now obliging Mrs Cooper – what excuse could he give her? Never mind, he would think of something – and contrive then to get a look round their places of residence, he might be able before the day was out to go to the Additional Commissioner.

But then the Dean had teasingly added that one extra thought.

'Inspector, I wonder if it has occurred to you that there might be another reason for someone to have taken that question-paper and handed it to that poor young man now in the KEM Hospital?'

Ghote had only just taken it in.

'Yes, sir?' he managed to say, halting in the doorway. 'Please, what it is you are suggesting?'

'Motive, Inspector. What I believe you police people call motive.'

'Yes, sir. Yes. Whatsoever reason a culprit has for committing offence under Indian Penal Code Section 352, murder, we are calling as motive.'

'Well then, Inspector, may I put it to you that forcing poor Bembalkar to resign so as to step into his shoes may not be the only reason, or motive, for taking that paper?'

Ghote allowed himself a moment to think, thankful that it was expected his reactions would be slow.

What was the Dean saying? Was he questioning the logic that had guided himself to believing that the person who had attempted to poison Bala Chambhar must be someone who wanted to become Principal of Oceanic College? But what other motive could the Dean have in mind? Yet – remember – the Dean, for all his evident enjoyment of spiteful teasing, was a clever man, one who had risen high in the academic world. So had he contrived to hit on something he himself had completely failed to see?

'Please,' he said, hardly having to put on an appearance of ignorance now, 'please what it is you are thinking?'

'Revenge, Inspector. Black and bloody revenge.'

'Revenge, Dean sahib?'

What could he be suggesting? Was this some film? Songs, dances and fights? Villains, heroes and vamps?

'Yes, Inspector, it has just occurred to me – I am putting it to you almost as the thoughts enter my head – that if someone in the college felt that he had been badly let down by Principal Bembalkar and if, immediately afterwards, the opportunity arose of taking that question-paper, the person I have in mind might have snatched at the chancc of revenge, Inspector.'

Could he be right? And who did he have in mind?

'Please, sir, you are stating and saying you are having some individual in mind. Please, what is the name of the individual in question?'

'But should I tell you, Inspector? I mean, thinking it over, I wonder whether I am being fair in perhaps impugning a respected member of the academic staff of this college.'

Ghote drew himself up.

'Sir, it is your bounden duty.'

'I thought you might say that, Inspector.'

The Dean gave a little wriggle of his plump body in his chair.

'Very well then, I shall do my duty. My bounden duty.'

'The name, sir?'

'Mr Victor Furtado, Inspector.'

It took Ghote only half a second to know whom the Dean was referring to. On the previous occasion he had been in this room the Dean had told him about the incident that had, as it proved, drawn Principal Bembalkar out of his office and caused him later to take an early lunch leaving his keys in his chamber door. A group of students, led as it happened by Bala Chambhar himself, had for some reason or other felt they had a grievance against one of their lecturers, a junior lecturer in English, and they had blackened his face. With some tarry substance.

His name was Victor Furtado.

Could what the Dean had suggested be right? Was Victor Furtado another suspect? It could be. Principal Bembalkar had altogether failed to stop that rag. So, if Victor Furtado as soon as he had at last been released, going perhaps to the Principal simply to complain, had found the chamber unlocked, had looked in and had seen the question-papers, it might well have struck him that by taking one he could pay out Dr Bembalkar for his failure to act with decision. True, revenge sounded unlikely as a motive for murder, more than a little filmi. But then it had not at the time been the motive for the near-murder of Bala Chambhar. It had been the motive only for snatching that Statistical Techniques question-paper and getting it somehow put on sale so as to bring maximum discredit to the Principal. The poisoning had been, surely, no more than a hasty effort to cover up the original impulsive minor crime.

So, yes, Victor Furtado could be his man.

'Sir,' he asked the Dean, 'are you by any chance knowing where this Mr Victor Furtado has his residence? I am thinking it would be one good idea first of all to eliminate him as a suspect, if at all possible.'

The Dean blinked behind his little gold-rimmed glasses.

'Do you think so, Inspector? Now, how are you going to go about that, I wonder.'

Ghote, who had just conceived the idea of searching Victor Furtado's residence in the hope of finding some evidence of a past purchase of Somnomax Five, thought it prudent not to say so.

'We are having our police methods,' he replied, conscious that such an answer to the Dean's probing, the best he could produce on the spur of the moment, was not likely to deflect him for long.

As it did not.

'I suppose your best plan,' the Dean went cheerfully on, 'might be to search Furtado's room – he occupies one in one of our student hostels, I believe – in the hope of finding some evidence of whatever poison was used on the wretched Chambhar? What was it exactly, Inspector? Have your astute inquiries already led you to that?'

A tiny dart of caution flicked into Ghote's mind. He had already told this mere unofficial assistant more than he ought. A good deal more, however useful he had turned out to be. But it would be better not to add to his indiscretions.

'Sir, my investigations till date have not revealed exact substance.'

'Ah, but you have something in mind?'

'Yes, sir.'

'Then let me direct you to Furtado's hostel. One must do everything within one's power to assist the police in their inquiries.'

'That is most good of you, sir.'

'It's not at all far from the college itself. I am sure that you will have no difficulty in finding it. A man of your courage and resource.'

'Yes, sir. Thank you, sir.'

'You go out of the college gate, Inspector, and turn to your left. Your left. Then you keep straight on till the first turning on your right. You understand? First a left, then a right?'

'First right – No, first left, then also right. Yes, sir.'

Did the fellow really believe a Crime Branch officer was incapable of remembering simple directions?

'And you will find the hostel – it is easily recognised – only some two hundred yards along.'

'Very good, sir. First right – '

'No, no. Inspector. First left. Left.'

'Oh, yes, sir. First left, then right. Thank you, sir. Thank you.'

Thoughts of the moment, if it should ever come, when he would be able to put his contemptuous informant properly in his place swirling round, he traversed the long corridors of the college. From each classroom in turn there came the sound of lecturers' voices, high-pitched and hectoring, as they dinned their various subjects into their students' heads.

His thoughts were abruptly halted, however, by a rolling burst of noise from the next classroom he was coming to. Laughter, jeering, some shouts even. Then its door was opened and a stream of students began to emerge, first boys then, slightly under protest, girls. Amid much laughter and bits of horseplay they headed away in the direction of the students canteen. Puzzled a little, he stood and watched.

Then, as the last of the students turned the corner ahead, he realised there was a sound still emanating from the classroom. The sound of a lecturing voice, though one much less vigorous and dominating than those he had heard earlier.

Curious, he went quietly up and peered round the still open door. But all he could see were the rows of student desks and benches, mounting up in tiers. And every seat was empty except in the farthest corner of the topmost row where a solitary girl, fat and bespectacled, crouched, furiously writing in a notebook.

In a moment he was able to make out clearly the thin, reedy voice of the invisible teacher.

' . . . makes us rather bear those ills we have than fly to others that we know not of? Thus conscience both make cowards of us all, and thus the native hue of resolution is sicklied o'er with the pale cast of thought.'

At that he recognised the words. Shakespeare. The very expression Principal Bembalkar had used describing himself. Sicklied o'er with the pale cast of thought. So that thin voice was reciting Shakespeare, and all his listeners, with the single exception of the fat girl taking notes – could she really be copying down, fast as she could go, just only Shakespeare's words? – had walked out on him.

Then he saw that, almost within three inches of his eye, there was a card in a brass holder on the half-open door. *Mr Victor Furtado MA*, it read.

He experienced a little jolt of shock. So here was the very man Dean Potdar had, only a few moments earlier, suggested to him as the man most likely to have attempted to murder Bala Chambhar.

Carefully he peered further round the door till he could catch a glimpse of the owner of the thin voice. He saw a young man, perhaps in his late twenties, with a full, fleshy Goan face on which there rested a pair of cheap plastic spectacles. Above his mouth, still slowly and almost expressionlessly reciting Shakespeare, there was a faint blur of moustache.

So this was Victor Furtado, possible murderer.

He certainly hardly looked the part. He was as far removed from the film villain that Dean Potdar's talk of revenge had conjured up as it was possible to be.

So what to do about him? Leave him to go trickling on with Shakespeare's words to that fat girl in the far corner? Dismiss him from all consideration, in fact? But a man might commit murder on a sudden, weak impulse as much as through long-matured dark plans. No, Victor Furtado at least merited questioning.

And why not now?

Not giving himself time for second thoughts, he stepped smartly in and marched up to his suspect.

'Mr Furtado?' he asked in a loud voice, easily over-riding the reedy pipe of 'Get thee to a nunnery: why woulds't thou be a breeder of sinners?' 'Mr Victor Furtado?'

Victor Furtado lifted his eyes from the book in front of him and brought his recitation to a trailing halt.

'Please? Yes?' he said. 'What is it?'

'Mr Furtado, I am a police officer, Inspector Ghote, Crime Branch, and I am wanting one word.'

'But – But – I am in the middle of giving out a lecture.'

Ghote turned and took a long look round the all but empty room. After a little Victor Furtado saw the point.

'Well, yes,' he said, 'some of my class has left. I have given permissions. If not in so many words . . .'

Suddenly he darted a look at the fat girl in the top corner.

'Miss Washikar,' he said, almost shouted. 'Kindly go. Class is dismissed. What for are you sitting and sitting?'

Miss Washikar scrabbled up notebook and handbag, and clutching both to her chest went rattling down beside the tiered benches and scuttled out.

'Police,' Victor Furtado said, glancing to left and right as if he too would have liked to have scurried out of the room. 'Please, what have I done that the police should be coming to me?'

'Well,' Ghote said, feeling moment by moment more aggressive faced with this whining fellow, 'suppose you are telling me what it is you have done?'

He stood fixing the Goan lecturer with an unyielding glare. Every inch the police officer well prepared to slap, and more.

Victor Furtado licked his lips.

'But – But – ' he said.

He gave a sudden look towards the door as if he was contemplating making a desperate run for it.

'But it was long ago,' he burst out unstoppably, his voice rising with every word. 'And I was explaining. In the end they were letting me go. I had done nothing. It was the others who were protesting.'

Ghote had no idea what he was talking about. But if his suspect was willing to confess, no matter what to, he was not going to let him off the hook.

'It is for me to be saying whether you had done nothing,' he snapped out.

Again Victor Furtado licked his lips.

'But many, many people were protesting also during Emergency days,' he said. 'And today all that is forgotten.'

'So,' Ghote banged back, 'you are one hothead, is it? Protesting and making troubles. We are well knowing what to do with such.'

'But, please, please, I have done nothing. My life has been so hard. It was once only I was protesting. Since then I have taken utmost care not to offend. Rather I have been a victim of protests by others.'

Ghote pounced. Surely the fellow had left the way open to bring up the very thing that had made him want to revenge himself against Principal Bembalkar?

'Victim, is it?' he said with piled-on scorn. 'I suppose next you will be telling you have been assaulted by your own students?'

'But, yes. Yes, that is what happened to me.'

Ghote gave a prolonged laugh.

'Oh, yes,' he said. 'A respected lecturer at the mercy of just only some students? Was it Miss Washikar from up there who was beating up and bullying you? Is it that you are expecting me to believe?'

'But it is true, Inspector. I am swearing I speak God's truth itself. It was not Miss Washikar, no. She is almost the only student who shows any respect. But it was the boys in this class. They blackened my face, Inspector. They did that itself, especially one Bala Chambhar.'

'Bala Chambhar?' Ghote leapt in again. 'Bala Chambhar who is even now lying in KEM Hospital on point of death. Death by poisoning. What do you know about that, Mr Victor Furtado?'

The look of blank fright that appeared on Victor Furtado's moustache-blurred face might well have been the look of a murderer about to confess.

'Poison,' he gasped out. 'But they were saying the boy was taking his own life.'

'That is what we were giving out, yes,' Ghote hammered on, allowing himself no time to think in the excitement of this sudden chase. 'But we know better than that, you and I, Mr Victor Furtado, isn't it?'

'No. No. No, no, no.'

'You are denying? You are daring to deny that first of all you handed to that boy a question-paper you had taken from Principal Bembalkar's chamber, hoping that selling copies of it would get him into damn serious trouble, but then fearing it would after all come out you had taken that paper you tried to poison Bala?'

'But – But, Inspector, how could I poison him? How?'

'Suppose you tell me. Suppose you tell me just exactly how you were attempting to get rid of that witness to your thieving.'

Victor Furtado's mouth opened and shut. No sound emerged.

Ghote allowed himself to feel he had, at almost the outset, hit on the truth of it all. But then Victor Furtado did manage to get some words out.

'Inspector, how could I have done that? I was no more seeing Bala Chambhar after he had – after he had done what he did to me. I was just only hearing some time later he had been taken to hospital.'

'Oh, yes? That I would believe when I am believing you can sweep the sky with a broom.'

'But it is true, Inspector. By Jesus, Mary and Joseph, it is true.'

Tears were beginning to creep down Victor Furtado's fleshy face from under his plastic spectacles.

Yes, it was possible he had his man under his thumb.

'Tell me,' he said, abruptly switching his line of attack, 'after they were blackening your face what was it you were doing?'

'Doing?'

Victor Furtado looked utterly bewildered.

'Yes, yes. Doing. You were not standing there under the Principal's balcony from that time to this, were you? So what was it you were doing?'

'I – I – I am forgetting.'

'No, you are not. Something like that does not happen to a person and he is passing it off as if it was just only a fly he had brushed from his face. Tell me exactly, and now only, just what it was you were doing when at last those boys left you in peace?'

'But – But – But what else should I do? I was attempting and trying to get that stuff off my face.'

With a thump of dismay, Ghote realised that this had all the sound of being the simple truth. Anyone whose face had been smeared with thick black stuff, thick and clinging, would want at once to get rid of it. And that would be a process not to be completed in five minutes. So what Dean Potdar had put into his mind, that picture of a furious Furtado, boiling with anger against Principal Bembalkar for failing to rescue him from the hands of his tormentors, going up there and then to complain and, when he found the Principal's chamber open and unguarded, stealing the question-paper as revenge, was, to say the least, unlikely.

Or was it? Certainly at first glance it would seem that Victor Furtado must have been busy scrubbing at his face for some considerable time, peeling away the sticky blackness. But just how long would that process have taken? How thorough had the fellow been over it?

He tried to put himself into the Goan's mind, to feel what he must have been feeling after that attack. Yes, his first instinct would have been to rid himself of the badge of shame. But, after he had made some efforts, what would he then have felt? Would he have been driven by an urge to remove every last trace of humiliation? Or would sudden despair have reached up at him? And then, face still smudged but more or less clear, what would he have done? Would he have gone to hide away somewhere? Or would he possibly then have decided to go to complain to Principal Bembalkar?

But, if he had, would he by that time have found the Principal back in his chamber, quite oblivious of the fact that in his absence and while his keys were carelessly left in the door, with Mrs Cooper not back at her customary post, someone had entered and had taken away that question-paper? Or would he have reached the office before the Principal had returned from that early lunch, while Mrs Cooper was still absent?

It was possible. Either account was possible.

Abruptly he made up his mind.

'Mr Furtado,' he said, 'I am requiring to examine your place of residence.'

13

Again the look of haunted fear came into Victor Furtado's eyes. But there was no deciding whether it was the active fear of a misdeed being found out or the more general fear of a man who seemed to go through life prey to every sort of anxiety.

'But, why, Inspector, why?' he bleated now. 'What are you going to find in the room that I have?'

'That we shall see,' Ghote replied. 'Kindly take me there.'

He marched Furtado half a pace ahead of him towards the entrance hall, deliberately keeping a grim silence in the face of the few pathetic attempts at speech the fellow made. But in the hall he encountered a check. Amar Nath was standing there, feet apart, hands behind his back, massive moustache curling, looking loftily at such students as were hurrying past. But at the sight of Ghote he had burst into life.

'Inspector, Inspector, I have important-important message.'

What the hell . . ?

He went over.

'Yes? What it is?'

Amar Nath felt in one of the pockets of his green uniform and produced an envelope, already battered and crushed.

'From hot-pant Cooper Mrs,' he said. 'Love letter, I am thinking.'

He was still laughing away when Ghote had finished reading the short note. *Station House Officer Dadar P.S. rang to say box in question cast on to dust heap.*

Inwardly Ghote cursed. A piece of hard evidence, something that could not but have impressed the Additional Commissioner. And in the time since he had visited Bala Chambhar's mother she had chosen to get rid of this reminder of her son at the point of death.

Well, he had better find some Somnomax Five with one or other of his suspects. Nothing less would convince the Additional Commissioner that the crime under investigation now was not the theft of one question-paper but murder itself. And Victor Furtado was still perhaps as good a bet as any as that would-be murderer.

Coming out of the college gate with him, Ghote was surprised to see the Goan turn unhesitatingly to the right and not the left. Surely Dean Potdar, in giving him his directions, had said he should turn left? He had said it twice even.

Was Victor Furtado planning flight?

He moved a little closer, ready to grab.

But his suspect showed no sign of taking to his heels, and before long they came to a side-road down which he turned as unhesitatingly as he had turned out of the college gate.

Ghote decided that either Dean Potdar in his effort to explain clearly to a thick-head police officer, had contrived to muddle himself, or that he, in his effort to appear a thick-head police officer, had got it wrong. Or had the Dean deliberately given him wrong directions as a malicious little joke? It was possible. Definitely possible.

The notion was confirmed less than two minutes later when Victor Furtado pointed to a tall water-stained barrack some two hundred yards ahead.

'It is there I am staying,' he said, with a glance half of fear, half of dim defiance.

'Very good,' Ghote answered tersely.

Evidently this must be the place. No attempt to cut and run on the part of his timid, sad-faced suspect. So, a joke of Dean Potdar's. Never mind, a day would come . . .

Then, as they neared the hostel a group of boys hanging out of one of its windows – why are they not in class? Ghote thought – started to whistle and shout at a girl in a red and orange sari walking by on the opposite side of the road.

'Oh, you beauty,' one of them called.

'Oh, yes, you bloody beauty,' another yelled.

Ghote felt a sharp sense of affrontedness. In his day no boy would have dared shout such words. Should he call up and tell them to behave?

He decided his business with Victor Furtado was more pressing. And then promptly wondered whether he was being any better than Principal Bembalkar when he had failed to stop the face-blackening beneath his balcony. Perhaps his own mistake now had been to think about what he should do. If he had acted straightaway, run ahead a few yards and given those riff-raffs a good reprimand, would they have learnt a lesson?

There was no telling.

But, worse, as they turned in at the hostel's wide, white-painted, rust-streaked metal gate – its top hinge had broken and it was leaning permanently open – the boys at the window began calling down directly to them.

'Hey, it is Furtado potato,' the first of them shouted in English.

'What you doing away only from your shaky-shaky-Shakespearing?' another called.

'Pinching the girls also,' a third voice joined in, this time in Marathi.

'Ignore them,' Ghote snapped, not that Victor Furtado was showing signs of doing anything else.

They stepped into the merciful shade of the entrance.

Boys like that should be beaten, Ghote said to himself, aware at once that he was enraged because he had failed to take any action.

As I have not taken action against Protima, he added with an inner twist of self-condemnation. Well, tonight . . .

But in the meantime he had more urgent things to do.

'Your room,' he snapped at Victor Furtado.

'Yes, yes, Inspector, we are going there.'

To Ghote's relief the lecturer's room turned out to be on a floor below the one where the boys had been leaning idly out of the window. At least he could get on with the business in hand uninterrupted by other concerns.

Victor Furtado took out a key and undid the padlock on his door. The room Ghote stepped into close behind him was almost as dispiriting as the man to whom it belonged, a narrow, bare rectangle, its walls painted pale green, peeling here and there. There was a low, iron-framed bed, above which on a sagging rope hung Victor Furtado's spare clothes with a sheet of newspaper pinned up behind to prevent the paint of the wall flaking off on to them. In front of the barred window there was a small table with two piles of tattered books on it and a wooden chair tucked under. Beneath the bed Ghote caught sight of an old suitcase.

Beyond that there was nothing.

'How long is it since you have stayed here?' he asked in dismay, before it occurred to him that he ought not to show such friendliness to his potential suspect.

'It is six years. Ever since I was getting my post here.'

'And you have not thought of shifting to somewhere better?'

'How can I, Inspector? I was having to find a big bribe to get the job, and I still have not paid back all I was borrowing.'

Yes, Ghote thought, as without asking permission he tipped over the two piles of books and, finding nothing, jerked open the drawer in the table, of course a fellow like Furtado would not get a post in a college such as this, however high his qualifications, without paying out to gain precedence over duller people with better connections.

'But you are married, no?' he asked, looking down into the drawer in front of him.

Really he must stop feeling sorry for this fellow. Damn it, he may well be the person who put that tub of luxury shrikhand in Bala Chambhar's way. That tub now gone for ever.

And yet would he have done? Would someone living as bare an existence as this have produced shrikhand from Monginis as bait for his victim? More likely it would be some wretched fried snack from a street vendor. And Bala, if he was as poor as that room in Chawl No 4 indicated, would most probably have gobbled that up. And, again, would someone as hard-pressed financially as Victor Furtado have a supply of American-imported Somnomax Five?

But that at least could soon be checked. He scrabbled the contents of the drawer to the front where he could see all there was.

And in the meanwhile Victor Furtado, sitting himself timidly on the edge of the bed and making no effort to protest at the way his table was being searched, was answering that careless question.

'Oh, yes, Inspector, I am married. I am very married. But how can I keep a wife here in Bombay? It is forbidden in the hostel. So, when I can afford it I go back to Goa in the holidays. Also I have to send her parents, where she stays, what I can when I earn a little from giving tuitions.'

Nothing in the drawer even resembling Somnomax Five. Nothing much in it at all. A few stubs of pencils, a half-used pad of writing paper, two curled-up aerogramme forms, a stub of eraser, half a dozen ballpoints all looking dried-up.

He turned to the suitcase under the bed, brushing it roughly against the Goan's dangling legs as he pulled it out.

'My pay is very low,' Victor Furtado went on, ignoring Ghote kneeling beside him ferreting through the contents of the suitcase, underwear, socks, a thread-pulled pullover, a single book *The Works of William Shakespeare*. 'And sometimes College is saying they must withhold salary for a month. Lack of funds. Once it was three months. And how am I able to live when they are doing that? Are they ever considering?'

Briefly Ghote thought of Mrs Rajwani. She must be very well-off, and yet it was worth her while apparently to be Oceanic College's Managing Trustee. There must be some money to be made running the place. Despite what they said they had had to do to Victor Furtado's monthly salary.

Ah, what's this?

Tucked away at the very bottom of the case, the flattened remains of a brightly printed cardboard box, its top torn away. Something that looked as if it might have contained a bottle.

Somnomax Five?

Could the fellow have been careless enough to have kept the outer container of the expensive preparation he had somehow acquired after using the stuff to poison the boy who could betray him as the question-paper thief?

The name of whatever had been in the bottle inside the box was missing. Peering hard in the insufficient light from the narrow window, Ghote examined the mass of tiny print still remaining.

Excessive generation of foul gases in the abdomen creates a feeling of heaviness even when very light food is taken. Low and loud sounds from different parts of the stomach, feeling of disturbance as though from pinpricks, feeling as though water moves inside the stomach, emanating gas attacking region of chest and growing pain –

Just some stuff for the stomach. Despite his disappointment, Ghote could not help reading on.

. . . feeling of being bitten by ants or traversed by insects, severe pain in different parts of the head, watering from the eyes, reduced or blocked hearing, bad dreams (experience of many people show that majority of gastric patients have sleep filled with bad dreams), intolerance to noise, desire to lie down always, fungus on the tongue, noxious odour in the mouth, insatiable thirst, bloodlessness, aversion to work, lack of thinking power.

Had Victor Furtado been attacked by all these unpleasant sensations? Or even some of them? To add to his other troubles. But at least those troubles did not appear to include his having impulsively stolen that question-paper and then having had to resort to murder to get himself out of it.

Or did they?

'Get up from the bed,' he snapped.

As soon as Furtado had obeyed, which he did without a murmur, Ghote heaved up the mattress – it was as thin as those he had seen in the KEM Hospital – shook it hard and felt it all over. But there was no sign of any concealed object. And nor was there now anywhere else to look in the little stone-floored room.

So, even if Victor Furtado was the person who had attempted to poison Bala, there was no hope of finding tangible evidence against him.

When it came to searching Professor Kapur's residence, if he could contrive to do it, would he have as little luck? Or at Mrs Gulabchand's? And if he was as unsuccessful, what could he then go with to the Additional Commissioner?

14

Ghote had felt when the affair had changed its object so dramatically that he was at least no longer that poor cat entrapped in the adage, if an adage was a trap and not something altogether different. With murder to be tackled, rather than the mere finding out how it had been that a wretched exam question-paper had been whisked out of a room apparently locked, he would be no longer a cat but a tiger. Yet now it seemed to him the adage was still there, only it had grown bigger, big enough to entrap any tiger. And yet more entangling. Could he ever fight his way out?

Gloomily letting this thought mill round in his mind, he made his way out of the hostel and turned in the direction of the college.

It was only when he became aware, as a vaguely apprehended sight, of a person some yards ahead suddenly switching from progress towards him to a rapid turning back, followed at once by a reversal of the process, that he realised he was meeting none other than Dean Potdar.

Was the little academic suddenly put out to find the joke he had played on his stupid police officer had not come off? And then had he decided to brazen it out?

'Why, Inspector Ghote,' the Dean greeted him, hurrying up. 'And without that deplorable young man Furtado. Has Sherlock Holmes failed to pin down his prey?'

Thoughts began to tumble through Ghote's mind. Stupid police officer, he must remember to keep that up. And he must be careful not to tell this civilian more about the case than he had to. Should he say anything about not finding any evidence in Victor Furtado's room? What had he said already about why he had wanted to search the place?

And what was all that about Sherlock Holmes?

He contrived at least to produce again the idiot grin he had found for the Dean before.

'Sherlock Holmes?' the little podgy fellow shot out at him. 'You're not acquainted with your illustrious, if fictional, predecessor?'

'Oh, yes, yes,' he answered, secure at least now in his dumb-ox role. 'Sherlock Holmes I am very well knowing. Master detective, no?'

'But has the master detective come away from young Furtado – I was told by our security officer you had left with him – without having discovered the perpetrator of – What was it? Ah yes, the diabolical plot?'

'Well, no,' Ghote answered, 'there is seeming to be no evidence that it is Mr Furtado who is the culprit only.'

He produced his grin again, beginning to feel a little proud of the air of bemusement it was surely giving him.

'Well, well, you cannot always hit on the arch criminal at first attempt. I seem to recall that even the great Holmes himself was sometimes wrong-footed.'

Ghote put on a baffled look at that.

'But, please,' he said, 'after not at all succeeding in finding one case against Mr Victor Furtado, I am very much wishing to go to the residence of either Professor Kapur or of Mrs Gulabchand. Are you by chance knowing their addresses?'

Dean Potdar's eyes brightened behind their little round gold-rimmed glasses.

'Better than that, Inspector,' he said. 'Mr and Mrs Gulabchand have a flat not too far from here. Allow me to take you there. You really ought to see if that lady is your wicked murderer.'

This was more than Ghote wanted. If the little fat man went round with him to wherever Mrs Gulabchand resided, he would want to stay no doubt while he conducted his search. Was he now going to become Sherlock Holmes to the Dean's Dr Watson and have him at his heels wherever he went?

'Please,' he said, 'I am not at all wanting to put you to troubles. If you will kindly inform me of the address, I would proceed there by myself alone.'

'Not at all, my dear fellow. Wouldn't think of it. Besides, the place is not easy to find, you know. Not particularly easy.'

The pompous piggy was doing it again. Did he really think a police officer who had risen to the rank of inspector would be unable to find one address in Bombay?

However, it seemed this particular police officer who had risen to the rank of inspector was unable to think of any good reason for rejecting the offer.

'You are one hundred percent kind.'

Together they walked back to the main road. It was stiflingly hot, and Ghote noticed that the Dean, who had looked uncomfortable tight-buttoned in his British-style tweed jacket even when he had come up to him, was now perspiring to a horrible extent.

'Dr Potdar,' he said, 'it is really too much to expect you to come in all this heat. I am sure I can easily find the Gulabchands' flat.'

'No, no,' the Dean said. 'You would never find it, I assure you. And look. Look, there's an auto-rickshaw.'

True, there was visible in the shade of a tree some hundred yards away an auto-rickshaw's yellow plastic hood.

'Come on,' the Dean said, 'or we'll find someone has come up and taken it.'

He set off, waddling along at a considerable rate. Ghote, following, wondered why the fellow was so keen to hire the little vehicle. If Mrs Gulabchand's flat was not far off there was surely no need to go by auto-rickshaw.

But as they sat side by side in the rattly machine – they had had to shake its driver awake from his noonday sleep across the vehicle's narrow back seat with his bare feet jutting into the air – he found the Dean's notion of 'not too far' was certainly different from his own. Despite the speed they were going at, rocking the light machine in a decidedly hazardous manner and sending fumes from its motor-cycle back to them in scorching waves, the trip went on and on. It was a full quarter of an hour before at last they reached Dhake Colony in Andheri, far south of the grim factory area of Oceanic College, and came to a halt.

By this time it seemed no longer worth going into why the Dean should consider their destination as being near at hand, something Ghote had not been able to ask about over the hammering noise of the auto-rickshaw engine. He looked around instead.

Mrs Gulabchand, he saw, lived in a prosperous apartment block, Ramaprakash Housing Society, with at its corner nothing other than a branch of Monginis cake shops. So would it be there that –

But he was given no time to ponder that. The Dean had trotted inside at a great pace, hurried over to the lift at the back of the narrow entrance hall and pressed its call button.

'You are knowing this place?' Ghote asked, taking in the Dean's familiarity with the lay-out.

'Yes, yes. The Gulabchands and I are on visiting terms.'

Ghote seized on the advantage this seemed to hold out.

'Then you would be able to go inside if no one is there excepting only a servant?' he asked, hoping he had made the inquiry sufficiently lacking in quickness.

'Yes, yes,' the Dean answered happily. 'So you see, Inspector, it has been worth your while after all availing yourself of my humble assistance. We shall have no difficulty in persuading the Gulabchands' servant, a simple fellow – you will like him – to let us in. Then you can search away as much as you like for whatever it is you are, very properly, not letting me know about.'

The lift arrived in front of them at that moment, and Ghote was able to conceal the jab of dismay he had felt at the acuteness of the Dean's remark.

In silence they went up to the fifth floor, got out and went to the door of the Gulabchands' flat. The Dean rang at the bell.

In a few moments the servant appeared, a patently thick-skulled fellow, mouth hanging open, eyes swivelling to and fro, smartly though he was dressed in a white uniform with a golden yellow cummerbund. Ghote could not decide whether he was pleased or not that, thanks to his tireless imitation of some sort of joke figure, the Dean had likened him to the fellow.

But at least the man's simplicity allowed the Dean to sweep them inside and on through a stuffily furnished drawing-room out to a balcony complete with two or three wicker chairs and a tall swing with a red plastic seat and bells attached to its ropes. Briskly the Dean ordered tea, something which, still sweating profusely, he plainly needed.

'Now, my dear fellow,' he said as soon as the servant had drifted off into the kitchen, 'off you go. Hunt, hunt, hunt. And, pleasant lady though Mrs Gulabchand is, I wish you the very best of luck – with whatever it is you need to find.'

Ghote felt a new jet of fury. Damn Dr Watson. Was he trying to take over the whole investigation? If such a tricky business as searching a flat without a warrant in the barest hope of locating a supply of Somnomax Five could be called an investigation. But, feel what he might, the chance of looking round the place was too good to miss.

After all, it was still generally believed that Bala Chambhar had attempted to commit suicide and, as far as anybody knew, the existence of that Monginis shrikhand tub had not come to light. So it was possible that whoever had crushed the sleeping tablets into the shrikhand had not felt it necessary to dispose of the remains of their supply. And the tablets might, in fact, have belonged not to Mrs Gulabchand but to her husband. So she might have used only as few of the pills as she thought would achieve her end. Too few it had proved. So some might very well still be here in the flat.

But where? Where exactly?

The bathroom. That would be the best bet.

Standing in the little hallway, oppressive with dark, richly-patterned wallpaper, dotted with bright specimens of tribal art and adorned with a tank of little brilliant swimming fishes, he could hear the servant banging away in the kitchen. So, rapidly one by one, he tried each of the doors beside him.

The third one he flicked open proved to be the bathroom.

He slipped inside. What if the tea was ready more quickly than they had counted on? Never mind, he could pretend he had needed to use the room. He slid the bolt on its door into place and turned to take a better look.

Yes, there was a mirror cabinet above the basin. He flipped it open. But it was soon clear, wherever else the pills might be, this was not the place. Two toothbrushes, one tube of *Neem* toothpaste. A razor. A tube of shaving cream. Three old razor blades stuck together with orange rust and a packet of new ones. The sole bottle contained only Mr Gulabchand's black hair-dye.

He looked round again. There was a cupboard under the basin. Could that be where sleeping pills were kept? He lowered himself to his knees, pulled open the door and stuck his head right inside.

Nothing but the pipes from the basin, a layer of gritty dust and, hanging from a hook, a pale pink plastic pourer which the Gulabchands must use at the lavatory bowl.

He got to his feet. First hope unfulfilled. There was certainly nowhere else in here where anything could be stored.

Was that a noise outside?

He froze.

Had the servant been quicker than he had thought possible with the tea? Well, if the fellow was outside he had his excuse ready, though then there would be no further search possible.

He slid back the bolt on the door. And, at the last moment, remembered to use the flush. Sweating slightly at the thought of how narrowly he had escaped making such a mistake, he waited for a count of ten and then opened the door. No sign of the servant. And clinking sounds and mutterings still to be heard from the kitchen.

So where now? Yes, the bedroom. The next most likely place.

But if the servant found him in there?

It had to be risked. The one advantage of his situation at the moment was that Dean Potdar, damn Dr Watson, was out on the balcony. So long as he remained there he would not see him illegally possessing himself of proof that Somnomax Five was present in the flat – if it was.

He slipped into the room he had seen was the bedroom. Not such an easy matter to search in here. In the bathroom there had been really only one place sleeping pills would be kept. Here they could be almost anywhere.

But most probably in one of the tables on each side of the heavily carved bed.

He hurried over to the nearer one, jerked the little drawer at its top open.

And there, there right in front, was exactly what he had been looking for. Not, as it happened, a bottle, but a small cardboard box, much smaller than the one that had once contained Victor Furtado's remedy for excessive generation of foul gases in the abdomen. And clearly labelled *Somnomax Five*. Inside there were three sheets of foil-wrapped tablets.

Hastily he slid one out, stuffed it into his trouser pocket.

Now, now he had hard evidence to take to the Additional Commissioner.

15

Ghote let Dean Potdar drink the tea the thick-skulled servant eventually brought. He felt he owed his Dr Watson that much. But, beyond at last admitting under more than a little eruditely joking pressure that, yes, his search had been successful, he evaded all the Dean's other questions, mostly by pretending not to understand a lot of what he was obliquely asked. Then, as soon as they had each finished a single cup, he announced that he must report urgently and hurried out, leaving the Dean plainly sharp with unsatisfied curiosity about what exactly it was he had found.

But, he thought as, having hailed a taxi and shouted 'Crawford Market', he made his way maddeningly slowly towards Headquarters, he still had not ended his contest with the little academic with even that much of a victory. Because, just as he had pulled the door of the lift closed in front of him, the Dean, standing at the Gulabchands' door, had shouted out something. He had not been certain with the clang of the lift jerking into motion whether he had heard what he thought he had. But it seemed the Dean had called 'But what if our other suspect also has a supply of – of whatever you found, Inspector?'

As the long trip from Andheri to Crawford Market wound its slow way, he asked himself time and again if that was what he had really heard. It seemed such nonsense. Somnomax Five was – he had Dr Shah's word for it – a new American prescription hardly sold at all in India. So how likely was it that two different members of the Oceanic College staff would each have a supply?

Ridiculous. Absolutely unlikely.

No doubt fat little Potdar was having one of his games with this supposedly dumb police officer. Of course, he was furious, this self-appointed Dr Watson, that he had not been confided in. And he was taking revenge.

But it all was yet another strand of hard-to-break fishing-line wrapped round the cat in the adage. If that was the way an adage was made. If that was what an adage was.

Yet the thought the Dean had plopped into his head, the absurd possibility, kept coming back to him until, at last, his taxi came in sight of the ancient British-built buildings of Headquarters.

Back in his own cabin, he asked at once to see the Additional Commissioner. Only to be told he was in conference. Feeling abruptly cut off from all that he had been doing since the moment he had been shown the report from the CBI team, he sat for some time at his desk doing nothing at all.

Then, as time passed, he found he was fighting a niggle of guilt about his actions in the Gulabchands' flat. To steal something that might well be evidence was hardly working by the rules he had abided by ever since he had passed out from Police Training School. True, he had left two other sheets of Somnomax Five behind. As soon as he got the green signal he could go, accompanied by the necessary witnesses, and conduct a pukka search revealing again the incriminating objects. But all the same he had acted rashly. Definitely.

But what if in the meanwhile Mrs Gulabchand made away with the evidence? Would that stupid servant have told her of his visit? No, after all the fellow did not know who it was who had accompanied the Gulabchand's friend, Dean Potdar. But Mr Gulabchand – Dean Potdar had told him he was Recreation Officer for, as it happened, the Bombay plant of Rajwani Chemicals – might he for some reason have decided to come home early and go to bed with something to make him sleep? And if he took every tablet remaining?

He shook his head angrily.

This was nonsense. No one was going to swallow that many sleeping pills. Not unless they did so unknowingly, as Bala Chambhar had done.

He looked at his watch.

When would the Additional Commissioner call him? Time was getting on. If he was to go back out to Andheri with two proper panches to witness him finding the Somnomax Five he ought to start getting hold of them soon. He would have to question Mrs Gulabchand, too. That might take hours. And, if he carried on into the depths of the night, in court when it came to the trial her pleader would allege she had been improperly pressured into making untrue admissions.

If she could be made to admit anything.

After all he had little to go on. Merely that he understood Mrs

Gulabchand wished to become Principal of Oceanic College and that she possessed or had access to the not widely available form of poison that had sent into a coma Bala Chambhar, to whom she might have passed on a question-paper stolen in order to embarrass the present Principal. No, it was a weak case. Unless Mrs Gulabchand succumbed to questioning.

And unless the Additional Commissioner summoned him soon there would be little likelihood of that happening tonight.

Still his telephone failed to ring. And still he found he lacked the heart to go back to such routine paperwork as he had outstanding.

Then at last the call came. He raced up the spiral stairs to the Additional Commissioner's office, peered hastily through the glass panel in its door to see if it was all right to enter, went in.

'Ah, Ghote, yes. Now, got that report to send to Delhi?'

'No, sir. No, that is – '

'Damn it, Inspector, you ask to see me. I make time for you in a hellishly busy day. And you tell me you have nothing to report.'

'No, sir. Yes, sir, I do have something to report. One murder, sir, I am thinking.'

Despite the icy glare that at once showed itself in the Additional Commissioner's eyes, Ghote plunged on with what he had to say. It did not take him long. And at the end of it he saw that the Additional Commissioner was, if anything, more coldly disapproving.

'Inspector, when I select an officer to prepare a report that can be sent to the CBI in Delhi, on a subject which has aroused the greatest interest at the highest levels, I do not expect to have to listen to a lot of rigmarole about the murder of some little anti-social in a slum in Dadar. Have you or have you not found out exactly how that question-paper got passed about through entire Bombay?'

'No, sir. Well, sir, not to one hundred percent, but – '

'Then get out there to that damned college wherever it is, Inspector, and find out. Do nothing else. Understood? If you've come across some evidence of a murder being committed – and it doesn't sound to me more than damned guesswork – then tell the victim's mother, if that's who it was you saw, to register a case with her local PS. Let them get on with it. But, as for you, what you tell me about an attempt to force the Principal of that place out there to resign may have something in it. Do I gather, however, that you've questioned neither of the damn professors involved?'

'Well, no, sir. No. I was following the line of Somnomax Five, sir, and – '

'Inspector, I do not want to hear one word more about that Somno-whatever-it-is. I want you to do what you have been told to do. Find out precisely how that blasted question-paper was on sale throughout Bombay. That and nothing else.'

'Yes, sir.'

Ghote returned to his cabin, hollow with dismay. He had known the murder case he had built up against Mrs Gulabchand was, at this stage, thin. But it had not somehow occurred to him that the Additional Commissioner would find it so weak. Or that he would be so enraged that it had delayed discovering what had happened to the Statistical Techniques question-paper.

But, damn it, he said to himself, a death, even of a harijan riff-raff like Bala Chambhar, is more important than satisfying someone in Delhi that no breath of scandal attaches to any partyman here in Bombay.

He knew, however, in higher circles different priorities existed. And he had been given orders, crystal-clear orders. So he must obey.

Yet even as he swallowed that sharp dose, a small hard bead of determination formed itself in his mind. If Mrs Gulabchand really had, simply in order to prevent her wretched plot against Principal Bembalkar coming to light, all but killed the boy Bala Chambhar, then she must not go unpunished. Yes, the Additional Commissioner had said Bala's mother ought to register a case. One hundred percent correct. In theory. But what would happen if she went to the local police taking with her no more than his own suspicions and conjectures? Even if she was capable of doing so much. Nothing. Nothing would happen.

No, if Mrs Gulabchand was to be brought to justice he himself was the person who would have to see that she was. And if that enmeshed him even more in some adage or other, well, let it.

So what to do now? Go back to the Gulabchands' flat and, if Mrs Gulabchand was there now, question her? Find out what she had been doing during the time Principal Bembalkar's keys had been dangling in his chamber door? The Additional Commissioner had been right to reprimand him for not having investigated that, though if his theory about murder had been accepted then surely he had been right to have done what he had.

But, no sooner had he seen what his first step should be than he realised he was not going to take it. In that bedside table in Mrs Gulabchand's flat there was the packet of Somnomax Five, the very substance used to poison Bala Chambhar. If he were to let her know this evening that he suspected her of taking the question-paper, the first thing she would do would be to get rid of that incriminating evidence of murder. No question any more of leaving the packet in its usual place so that its disappearance would not alert her husband, who since she had not taken all the tablets must be the one who used them. No, now she would seize the first opportunity to get rid of the whole pack. She would have to, at any risk.

Nor would he himself be able to prevent her. He had been specifically ordered not to pursue the case of attempted murder. Even if he succeeded in getting Mrs Gulabchand to confess on the spot to having taken the question-paper, and he doubted very much whether he would be able to do that without better evidence to confront her with, that crime was hardly so grave that he could march her off straightaway to a cell.

But, he thought, he would not strictly be disobeying the Additional Commissioner if he omitted to question Mrs Gulabchand tonight. He had been told to investigate both contenders for Principal Bembalkar's job. So if he happened to go to Professor Kapur first that was a matter of simple chance. Mrs Gulabchand could, in fact, safely be left till tomorrow when he could tackle her at the college. Then she would not find it so easy to rush back home and dispose of those tablets.

He hauled his copy of the Bombay telephone directory up on to his desk and riffled through the pages till he came to the long list of Kapurs. But eventually he found Prof D.R. Kapur. The address was in far-off Malad not far from Oceanic College. It would be another long, hot miserable journey with the rush hour now well under way. But he would have to go.

And, besides, he thought fleetingly as he left his cabin, though this was an evening when he could expect Ved with his new responsibilities as captain of the Regals not to be at home, he had not yet settled in his mind just how he was to set about the business of beating his wife. So it was as well to postpone all that.

Professor Kapur's flat, when at last he reached it, though it was in a block not outwardly much different from the Gulabchands', was very different inside. The servant opened the door on to a noticeably bare hallway. Its single table bore only a single battered-looking book, evidently left there and forgotten. A row of chappals was lined up against the opposite wall. Nothing else. The servant was, equally, quite different from the Gulabchands' smartly dressed if thick-headed fellow. This young boy – he was perhaps no more than twelve or thirteen – looked as if he had come straight from the melon fields.

However, after he had hastily joined his shoes to the row of chappals, the boy succeeded in announcing him to his master well enough. The professor's room had, like the Gulabchands' drawing-room, a good many books in it. But with the preponderance of ancient, wide-leaved astrological works and the absence of chairs and anything resembling a television set it was in no way western.

Nor was Professor Kapur himself, a burly squat figure in all-white kurta and dhoti, the grey hair on his bullet head cropped almost out of existence, chin and cheeks covered with a bristly grey stubble, anything of a western figure like Dean Potdar or Principal Bembalkar.

At Ghote's entrance he had contented himself with just glancing up from the low takht on which he sat cross-legged.

'Inspector Ghote,' he said. 'Potdar Sahib was explaining to me that you had been sent to the college. But I can tell you all your good endeavours will come to nothing.'

Ghote stiffened.

'Thorough investigation will always uncover the truth,' he said. 'So why should you state and claim I will not succeed.'

'The stars, Inspector. There it is written. There is a fate which cannot be avoided.'

A bristle of irritation went through Ghote. His feelings about astrological predictions were, he knew, mixed. He had never seen them as a substitute for good, hard, scientific police work. He even tried always to ignore them in his daily life, although Protima relied on them in conducting much of her affairs, and his. But then, too, he had never been able quite to push aside the residue of all that he had learnt at his mother's knee and from the stars-guided life of the village in which he had spent his earliest days.

He was damned, though, if he was going to accept a prediction handed out to him as Professor Kapur's had been. One based on no knowledge of his date of birth or the lines on his hand or any other of the factors an astrologer was supposed to work with.

'Stars or not at all stars, sir,' he said, 'I must continue the inquiries it is my duty to make.'

Professor Kapur gave him a tiger-like grin.

'Continue, continue, Inspector,' he said. 'But you would be better, I am telling you, to surrender.'

'Surrender?'

Ghote felt himself at once in battle position.

'Yes, Inspector, to surrender. Surrender to destiny, to the timeless pattern. It is there. You cannot escape it.'

'Are you saying, sir, you will not answer the questions I am here to put? May I remind it is an offence against Indian Penal Code, Section 179 itself, to refuse to answer a public servant authorised to question.'

'No, Inspector, put each and every question you are wishing and I will answer if I can. All I am saying is you will be altogether wasting your breath.'

'That we would see. First, please, where were you yourself on Monday last between the hours of 12.30 and 2 p.m.?'

He had not intended to put a question as challenging as this. Thinking about what he would say on his way out, he had seen himself conducting what he was convinced, in view of what he knew about Mrs Gulabchand's Somnomax Five, need be no more than the merest formality of an interview. He would begin with a few general queries about the routine of life at Oceanic College at midday. Then he would ask if the professor had happened to be in the vicinity of the Principal's office round that time and had by chance noticed anyone there. But the stifling blanket of astrology that had been thrown at him had driven all such polite nothings from his mind.

And, to his surprise, his question appeared to catch Professor Kapur at a disadvantage. He blustered.

'I was – I – What for are you asking me this? Are you attempting to say that I was the person who stole that question-paper or whatever it was from the Principal? It is well known that that was done by that harijan boy, Chambhar. How dare you try to accuse me of that.'

What was this? Why was the fellow suddenly so defensive? Why had he taken that question as a direct accusation?

The thought of what Dean Potdar had called out from the doorway of the Gulabchands' flat came back. It was, after all, not against strict logic for more than one person to have a supply of Somnomax Five. However much it was against probability that each of the two contenders for Principal Bembalkar's seat should possess this particular brand of foil-wrapped, blue-printed American sleeping pills. So could Professor Kapur just possibly be, not a person he was duty bound to go through the formality of interviewing, but a genuine suspect?

Yes. Just possibly, yes.

He thought rapidly.

'Sir,' he said, 'I am not at all accusing. But it is the duty of an investigating officer to consider each and every possibility. So I am asking once again: where were you between 12.30 and 2 p.m. last Monday, the time when that question-paper was removed from Principal Bembalkar's chamber?'

Professor Kapur glared up at him.

'I can assure you, Inspector, I was not anywhere near that chamber.'

'I am pleased to hear. But kindly tell where it was that you were?'

'No.'

'No?'

'No, Inspector, I am not going to tell you. It must be sufficient that I have said I was not in or anywhere near the Principal's office.'

Ghote drew in a breath, and, without thinking how much it would be wise to say, plunged in.

'No, sir. That is not sufficient. Let me explain. That question-paper – it was in Statistical Techniques – was not stolen from the Principal's chamber by the student Bala Chambhar although he was known to have sold copies in many places in Bombay. It could not have been. Of that I have made certain. The paper was taken by some other person, and that person later made sure it fell into the hands of Chambhar. That person's object can only have been to discredit Principal Bembalkar. Sir, this was in order to make certain Dr Bembalkar would resign, resign to make way for someone else.'

He saw a look of calculation come on to the astrologer's heavy round face in place of the contemptuous anger that had shown itself there till now.

'You are thinking, Inspector,' he said slowly, 'that I am that person? That I took that paper so as to discredit that westernised fool Bembalkar and step into his seat where I could bring to Oceanic College more of respect for the ancient art I teach and practise?'

'Yes, sir, I have to take such into account as one possibility.'

Professor Kapur gave a grunt of acknowledgement.

'Well, to this extent you are right,' he said. 'I will become Principal of Oceanic College. Such is written in my horoscope.'

For an instant Ghote quite failed to take in what Professor Kapur had said. The words had been spoken with no more emphasis than the astrologer had put into anything he had previously said, though he had been vigorous enough. But after that instant the full enormity of the statement came home. The man had stated that nothing could prevent him succeeding Principal Bembalkar because such was written in his horoscope. Because of some scratchings and scrawlings on a palm leaf based on abstruse calculations stemming from the position of the distant circling stars at the time of his birth he simply believed that the post would become his. It was monstrous. Monstrous. However much some things he himself had known to be foretold had come disconcertingly to pass.

He swallowed. Once. Twice. And then brought himself to speak.

'Sir – Sir, I am asking once again: where was it that you were on Monday between the hours of 12.30 p.m. and 2 p.m.?'

A glint of anger seemed to be the only response.

But then, after a moment's silence, the astrologer produced an answer.

'Inspector, why cannot you understand? It is no use you asking such a question. It is my fate to become Principal of Oceanic College, so what for should I plot and plan to achieve it? It is written. It will happen. It is good for me, but that is unimportant. I cannot change it, any more than men who writhe and twist under a bad fate can change that. It is there. There in the pattern above.'

Ghote felt as if a huge wall of rock had appeared in front of him. Immovable. Here was this man who simply believed, mistakenly or not, that sooner or later he would become head of Oceanic College. He had needed, so he had said, to take no decision to seek the position. He had not needed to weigh up what he should or should not do. He had only to stay still and let the giant wheel of fate move on till he had reached what he saw as his destiny to achieve.

So would such a person put into action a plan to discredit the man who held for the time being the post he was, so he believed, sure to inherit? Would he even, faced with the sudden opportunity of taking that question-paper and discrediting the man whose duty it was to keep it under locks and keys, have acted on impulse, as whoever had taken the paper must have done? The answer could only be no.

But could that claim of his be accepted at face value? To that the answer was much less clear.

And why was he refusing to say where he had been at the time of the theft?

'Sir,' he said yet again, 'you would be making my task much easier, yours also, if you would say where you were when that question-paper was stolen.'

'Private business, Inspector.'

Was the fellow saying that he had been behaving in some disgraceful manner sexually? Was it written in his horoscope that he was allowed all sorts of depravities at that certain hour?

Only one way to find out. Ask.

'Sir, I am a police officer. I am very much well acquainted with all the things that – that certain appetites can lead men into wanting and doing. Sir, you may be speaking freely in front of me.'

He stopped. Had he said enough?

A moment later he knew he had. Or had said too much. The look of bull-like rage that flooded up into the astrologer's grey-stubbled face as he came to understand what had been said to him made that altogether clear.

'Get out. Get out of my house. I will not sit and hear such abuses. Leave at this instant.'

Damn. Utterly defeated, whichever way you looked at it. Either he had succeeded truly in insulting this professor of astrology, an innocent and perhaps influential man, or he had been put in a position whereby he could not get an answer to his hundred percent legitimate question.

Only thing now to leave. With whatsoever of dignity he could manage.

'Very well, sir. If you are continuing to refuse to answer, I would let matter rest. But I must be warning you. I shall come back.'

He walked out. The servant boy was not in the bare hallway. He stooped to gather up his shoes. But then, suddenly seeing himself crouched down on the floor with the astrologer perhaps coming suddenly out to make sure he had left, he rapidly straightened up and with a foot slid the shoes over towards the table where he could stand upright and have something to lean on as he slipped into them.

He got his right foot safely into its shoe and then began to ease his left foot in, all the while keeping half an eye on the door of the room behind him.

So it was only as he wriggled the second shoe comfortable that he took note of the old book lying on the table in front of him. Something silvery had been used as a mark in its pages. It seemed somehow familiar.

But he dismissed it from his mind. He hardly wanted Professor Kapur to come out and find him apparently peering at one of his astrological works.

He turned to the flat's door. And, as he did so, it came to him just what that silver of a bookmark was.

A piece of blue-printed foil such as he still had in his pocket. Foil from Somnomax Five.

16

For a moment Ghote stood still at the door of Professor Kapur's flat, transfixed by what he had just seen. Then, on an almost involuntary impulse, he shot out and slammed the door behind him. On the landing he came to a halt again, heart thumping, and thought.

So, had the logical but highly improbable possibility proved true? Was each of the apparent heirs to Principal Bembalkar in possession of a supply of the poison that had all but ended Bala Chambhar's life? Plainly they were. With his own eyes he had seen that packet of Somnomax Five in the bedside table in the Gulabchands' flat. One of the full foil slips was in his pocket at this very moment. Equally with his own eyes he had seen what looked to be the foil wrapping from a sheet of Somnomax Five used as a bookmark in a neglected astrological volume belonging to Professor Kapur. And if he had failed to take a sample of it, that was perhaps all for the best. He could not go on flouting the rules of investigation at every turn. It was enough that he knew evidence of Professor Kapur having been in possession of Somnomax Five existed.

But now surely a different complexion altogether had been put on what he knew. What he knew and had been forbidden to act upon directly. Now it was likely, all too likely in his own view, that either Mrs Gulabchand or Professor Kapur had put a tub of shrikhand in the boy's way with tablet after tablet of Somnomax Five crushed into it. Either of them could have pretended to come across the boy while they were carrying the shrikhand, and, as if on impulse, have given it to him saying they no longer wanted it. Ever hungry, he would not have thought twice about taking it.

But which? Which of them had done those things?

And how could he go about proving, one way or the other, first, in accordance with his strict orders, that either Oceanic College's professor of astrology or the head of its English Department had taken that Statistical Techniques paper from the Principal's chamber? And then later, if he could arrange matters, how to prove that same person had also attempted to murder Bala Chambhar?

God, that adage had doubled in tangled criss-crossings now. He found he could even distinctly recall the old notebook in which, in his larger schoolboy hand, he had written that careful note. *Adage* =. But what? That last word remained completely blank in his head.

But one thing, he realised, was at least clear. It was too late today to do anything. He would not now get home till a late hour – Protima would be asleep, all unknowing of what he planned for her when he had time – and first thing in the morning he would have to go back out to the college once more. Perhaps he might then try yet again to take further advantage of Dean Potdar's twinkling contempt of himself to learn something that would help. He could not at the moment see any other way of extracting himself from his terrible tangle.

So once more he made his way homewards through the mostly sleeping eight-millions mass of Bombay's inhabitants. Once more he arrived to find only darkness. Once more he crept to bed hoping not to disturb his wife. And once again he swallowed a hurried breakfast before setting off early to repeat nearly the same journey in the other direction.

But as he arrived a little later than he had meant to be at Oceanic College, thinking with a quick sweat of dismay how much longer than expected his investigation into the missing question-paper had already taken, he felt that something was oddly different about the place.

It actually took him several seconds to realise what it was.

The quarter-mad South Indian cycle-stand attendant Krishna Iyer, MA Madras, was not in his place. Nor were there any students cramming round the stand to put their machines away. There were, in fact, no students to be seen anywhere. Not a single one. And, though the wide doors of the college building were standing open, even Security Officer Nath was not marching about just inside demanding to see identity cards.

Only when he himself entered the building did he discover what had happened. The blackboard he had seen the first morning he had come here, with its notices about enrolment, had been set up, this time just inside the building. But it bore now, in boldly chalked letters, just one announcement. *Day of Mourning for Late Sant Shankarananda College Patron No Classes.*

He was surprised. Nothing had been said to him, by Mrs Cooper, by Dean Potdar, by Principal Bembalkar or anybody else, about a total shutdown. Yet surely if a Day of Mourning was to be held it must have been decided on long ago. Perhaps it was an annual event. So there ought to have been plenty of warning. Yet this board with its message had not even been in place the morning before.

He shrugged. Unaccountable.

But would Dean Potdar, or anyone else, be here for him to ask about the time of the question-paper theft?

Slowly he climbed the deserted stairs to the offices on the first floor. The absence of any students, hurrying up them, running down them, standing in clusters on them blocking the way, laughing, larking, arguing, gave him a feeling of odd unease. So he was much relieved, as he turned the corner on to the long veranda outside the offices, to see Dean Potdar himself standing, black-gowned and formal, looking down on to the empty courtyard below.

'Good morning, sir,' he greeted him briskly, forgetting in his state of puzzlement to put on his show of stupidity.

Luckily the Dean did not seem to register his more alert air.

'Good morning, Inspector,' he said. 'I am surprised to see you here, though. Can it be that you have still made no arrest in the course of your dynamic investigation?'

The joking tone was warning enough.

'Oh, sir,' he said, wagging his head like an idiot, 'no such luck in all my inquiries till date. No such damn luck whatsoever.'

'So you have come back here, Inspector, eh? But I'm sorry to have to tell you if you are looking for dear Mrs Gulabchand to interrogate in your customary merciless way, or even if you are looking for that good fellow Kapur – Professor Kapur, of course, I should say – then you will be unlucky. This is our Day of Mourning, you know.'

'Yes, sir, I was seeing. In the entrance hall. The board.'

'Ah! You noticed that, Inspector? Well done, well done. Let no one say our police officers are lacking in powers of observation.'

'Yes, sir,' Ghote said.

Within he felt an intense longing for the moment when he would be able to show this pompous little man just what a Bombay Crime Branch officer could do. But it seemed plainer than ever that to get the most out of a highly useful source of information there was nothing for it but to go on playing at being altogether brainless.

'But, please,' he said, 'what is this Day of Mourning? I was not at all hearing of same yesterday only.'

Dean Potdar's eyes behind his gold-rimmed pince-nez twinkled with delight at this.

'Ah, Inspector,' he said, 'there was a very good reason for that.'

'Yes, sir?'

'You see, Inspector, the Day was decided on just yesterday itself. And I wonder if you can guess why.'

Ghote knew what was expected in answer to that.

'Oh, no, sir, not at all. I am not having one faintest idea.'

The Dean's round face creased in redoubled merriment.

'Inspector,' he said, 'did you know that it was today that the University of Bombay in its almighty wisdom has chosen to send to lowly Oceanic College an LIC?'

Ghote nearly betrayed the fact that he had heard from Mrs Cooper that an LIC was a Local Inquiry Committee, and that he had in fact been aware that such an investigatory team was due at the college.

But he was just in time.

'Please, what is LIB?'

'LIC, Inspector. LIC.'

The Dean sounded waspishly annoyed that this joke of his, whatever it was, was in danger of being spoilt by police stupidity.

'Oh, yes, sir, LIC I was meaning to say same.'

'Yes. Well, an LIC, Inspector, is an inquiry, consisting generally of two or three senior university administrators, appointed to look into conditions at any of the many constituent colleges in Bombay University where there appears to be cause for concern.'

'Oh, yes, sir.'

'And, oddly enough, it has been felt at the highest level in the university that Oceanic College now comes within that definition.'

'They are sending this inquiry team to here?' Ghote asked, best idiotic fashion.

'Worse, Inspector. They have sent it. The august investigators are expected shortly. Hence our Day of Mourning.'

Ghote saw it. But knew better than to let that appear.

'But, sir,' he said, 'if it is a Day of Mourning and there are no classes, there may be nothing for this LIB – this LIC to witness.'

'Exactly, Inspector.'

Ghote left it for a few seconds for this subterfuge to sink in to a simple police officer's mind. At last he produced, not without difficulty, a guffawing laugh.

'Oh, jolly good, jolly good.'

Then he let his face fall.

'But is no one besides your good self here?' he asked. 'Will I be able to see nobody?'

'Well, no, Inspector, you will not. My teaching colleagues have, of course, seized the opportunity of doing no work. However, the Principal is in his seat, needless to say, should you wish to see him and his faithful Mrs Cooper is naturally there as well.'

Well, another talk with Mrs Cooper might be worth having. Perhaps she would be able to tell him if anybody had been due to have come up to the Principal's office just after midday last Monday.

'Oh, most good,' he said. 'I will talk with Mrs Cooper. She is always very, very helpful.'

'Yes, Inspector, a most helpful lady.'

The Dean looked at him for a moment through his little gold-rimmed glasses.

'Yes,' he added with a little jump of abruptness. 'Most helpful, and devoted, of course, to poor Bembalkar's interests. Almost too much so at times, I sometimes think. You know, of course, that Bembalkar lost his wife some months ago?'

'Please?'

Dean Potdar took him by the elbow and led him away a few yards along the balcony.

'I can see I shall have to acquaint you with some of the facts of life, Inspector,' he said.

'Yes, please?'

The Dean let go his elbow and twisted his podgy little hands together.

'I suppose things of this sort never occur in police circles, Inspector,' he said. 'But in the groves of academe, as we call them, I regret to have to say relations between the sexes are not always as chaste as our great Hindu epics teach us they should be, in so far as they do. So it could well fall out, you see, that even a widowed lady like the good Mrs Cooper might conceive a terrible passion for someone – someone, shall we say, like our friend Bembalkar. Now, while Bembalkar was decently married I am sure that nothing, nothing remotely untoward, passed between those two. But now, don't you see, Bembalkar is what we might call a loose card. And it is possible – mind, I say no more than that – it is possible that our Mrs Cooper may feel tempted to gather that card into . . . What do you think of the expression "her ample bosom", Inspector?'

For a moment Ghote was genuinely at a loss for a reply. He really needed as much time to think about what the Dean, clearly, intended to put into his head as a stupid police inspector would be expected to take to work out what had been meant. That Mrs Cooper might, for some reason springing from an illicit passion for Principal Bembalkar, have hit on the idea of discrediting him and so secure his resignation.

And that was possible. If Mrs Cooper had been telling him the truth about Dr Bembalkar's frustrated desire to quit his difficult post and devote himself to his as yet unstarted book on *Hamlet*, then was it not likely that she would take this roundabout way of helping him? Or, if not likely, at least just possible? Perhaps, even, when Dr Bembalkar was no longer a dignitary of the college she might have some notion of joining him as his wife.

'Please,' he said hastily, since the Dean must be expecting some response, 'I am not very well understanding.'

'No? Then let me put it in words of one syllable. Inspector, has it occurred to you that Mrs Cooper is in love with Bembalkar? And we all of us know Bembalkar would quit his post in an instant if Mrs Maya Rajwani, our revered Managing Trustee, who thinks she has him nicely under her thumb, would let him. So can it be that Mrs Cooper has taken a somewhat extraordinary step to help Bembalkar out of his situation?'

The Dean may not have exactly used one-syllable words, Ghote thought, but he certainly has not hesitated to make matters altogether plain.

But was he possibly right? It really seemed a very unlikely thing for anyone to do.

Except a person truly gripped by sexual desire. Someone like that might do anything regardless of the consequences and often against all that ordinarily was expected of them. And there was this, too. No one could have easier access to Principal Bembalkar's chamber than his secretary. Mrs Cooper could have taken that Statistical Techniques paper far more easily than either of the other two he suspected.

Yes, this was another factor altogether.

Another strand round the adage.

Of course, Mrs Cooper had no Somnomax Five. Or was even that so? Ridiculous, absurd, as it might sound, it was still possible that like Mr Gulabchand and like Professor Kapur she did not sleep well. And, come to think of it, though at first glance it seemed altogether ridiculous that three people at the same college should each have sleeping pills that were not on wide sale in Bombay, were most likely smuggled, it was quite possible that the tablets had been recommended round the senior common room. Say Principal Bembalkar himself had tried them, and had talked about them to his secretary. He might even have given her part of his own supply.

The thing to do – it came to him suddenly – was to talk again to Principal Bembalkar, find out what he thought about Mrs Cooper, whether he trusted her, whether he had ever had any cause not to, and perhaps whether, now a lonely widower, he ever thought of her as more than his efficient guardian secretary. And even to ask him if he had ever given her any sleeping pills.

No sooner thought of than done.

'Well, well, I must not stand here idle all the day,' he said to Dean Potdar. 'At least I can make some inquiries now that I have come all the way to here.'

He knew that the Dean would be delighted to see him go off so promptly once a new suspect had been put in front of him in the way a cat – and he was, or was he, a cat, a cat in an adage? – will lie a mouse in front of its owner. But all the better if this still increased in the Dean's mind that picture of himself as the simple police officer. There might yet be more he needed to find out from the fellow.

He heard the clatter of Mrs Cooper's typewriter before he even opened the door to the Principal's outer office, and when he entered he found her, wearing today not her customary red blouse but a white one, hammering hard at her machine.

'Good morning,' he said. 'I am wishing to see Principalji. Is he free only?'

Happily the guardian rakshas was smiling when she answered.

'I will tell him you are here. I do not think he would make any difficulties. As it is a Day of Mourning, I have had to cancel all his engagements.'

She pressed the switch of her intercom and a moment later Ghote was again facing Principal Bembalkar across his wide table with its rack of well-used pipes. But today the Principal was not protecting himself by sucking and sucking emptily at one of the pipes. Behind his carefully knotted necktie and heavy-rimmed spectacles, he looked a distinctly more decisive figure than when he had confessed to having failed to lock his chamber door on the day that the Statistical Techniques question-paper had been stolen.

'Sit, sit, Inspector,' he said. 'Tell me how your investigation is proceeding. I am able to give you more of my time today.'

Suddenly and unexpectedly he chuckled.

'Yes,' he said, 'thanks to our Day of Mourning, our rather suddenly arranged Day of Mourning, I am, as you might say, quite at a loose end.'

Ghote found himself a little disconcerted. Going into the Principal's chamber, he had briefly recalled the beaten and bowed-down man who had admitted at last that he had allowed that question-paper to be taken from him. So to find someone now so bouncingly cheerful and cock-a-hoop was a considerable surprise.

He would have to think again about the way to approach his relations with Mrs Cooper.

To give himself time to adjust he spoke about the Day of Mourning.

'I was somewhat surprised to find the college shut down just now,' he said. 'I had hoped to find many persons here who could answer my questions. When I was leaving here yesterday I was not at all seeing this Day was to take place.'

Again Principal Bembalkar chuckled.

'No, Inspector,' he said. 'You see we arranged the whole thing at very short notice. We were saddled with an LIC, a Local Inquiry Committee you know. Quite unnecessary. Quite unnecessary. And so, acting on Mr Potdar's advice, I decreed this mourning day. A shrewd fellow Potdar. Our Dean, you know. You have met him of course?'

'Yes, sir. Yes. He has been most helpful to me.'

'And to me, Inspector, and to me. I am thoroughly grateful I took his advice. Perhaps a somewhat cunning move, even a little underhand. But effective. Effective.'

He leant back in his chair.

'You know,' he said, 'there are times in this world when one has to act with decision. Yes, decision. Even with ruthlessness. A touch of ruthlessness. It is the only way to get things done. Yes, to get things done.'

This was a new aspect of the Principal. And one that Ghote felt somehow was not altogether right. Perhaps, ashamed of his lack of decisiveness when Victor Furtado had had his face blackened in the courtyard right outside his office and all that had followed from that, he had swung wildly in the other direction.

It seemed, too, that happy bravado was not a permanent state. Hardly had he finished his chant of praise for effective action than behind the dark frame of his spectacles a look of caution came into his eyes.

'Yes,' he said, reaching for one of his pipes, 'but there is one thing, Inspector.'

'Yes, sir?'

'I don't know how well you have been getting on with my secretary. I gather she has been able to help you once or twice.'

'Yes, sir, she has been altogether helpful.'

'Yes. But let me warn you, Inspector. Not a word to her about – about what I have just mentioned to you. These things need to be kept *sub rosa*, as we used to say when I was a student in the UK. Yes, *sub rosa*. Under the rose. Not talked about. Potdar was most insistent on that. And quite rightly. Quite rightly.'

Ghote felt a small spurt of pleasure. He had been debating with himself how to bring the talk round to the subject of Mrs Cooper without making it evident that she was possibly a suspect in the question-paper theft, and now the Principal had done it for him.

'Oh, no, sir,' he said quickly. 'I am assuring you I would never mention such to any persons whatsoever. Not even to Mrs Cooper, though I am supposing she is somewhat in your confidence. There must be matters she is knowing that should not be told to each and every person in the college.'

Principal Bembalkar looked a little uneasy.

'Well, yes, of course,' he said, 'one's secretary has to know things that one would not necessarily wish . . . wish all and sundry to have knowledge of. There are letters to be typed et cetera. Files to be kept in order. But nothing that I am told in strict confidence goes beyond these four walls, Inspector. Nothing at all.'

Principal Bembalkar looked round at the wood-panelled walls of his chamber with an air of rectitude.

'Not that I do not have complete confidence in Mrs Cooper,' he said. 'She has been with me ever since I was appointed to my position, and I have never had a moment's doubt about her. But there are certain matters which even the most discreet of secretaries should not be privy to. Mrs Maya Rajwani would be – well, there are these matters, as I have said.'

'Yes, sir. I am sure Mrs Cooper is just as you are saying. She is a widow, is she not?'

He felt a little lift of delight at the adroit way he had reached that point.

'Yes, yes. She is, poor woman. She was left a child, a small child. That is why she needs to work.'

'Yes, sir. I am sure she is having a very hard life. Is she fit and well, sir? Does she have sleepless nights and so forth?'

A bloom of pure pleasure welled up in him at the neatness with which he was pursuing the subject.

'Sleepless nights, Inspector? I am sure I don't know. With a small child . . . I suppose she must have done at times. But she has never mentioned anything like that to me. Not that I remember.'

'No, sir.'

A disappointment. If Mrs Cooper had had access to Somnomax Five, it clearly had not been through her boss. Nor did it seem he knew too much about his secretary's life. Perhaps there was nothing after all in that malicious suggestion of Dean Potdar's. No doubt many of the things that fellow said were nothing more than malice.

He drew in a breath, took a quick decision.

'Sir,' he said, 'I must ask you this. It is my duty, as you know, to find out who it was who was coming into this chamber and taking that question-paper. It is a duty even to the extent of sending my report to the Centre itself. So, sir, there is no getting past this. One of the people who could have come in here and done that must be your trusted secretary, Mrs Cooper.'

He saw from the look on the Principal's long, lugubrious face that this thought had never for a moment entered his head.

But what did that mean? That he was altogether an academic with no knowledge of the world and its ways? Or that he did know Mrs Cooper well and was certain she could not be the question-paper thief? Or that she had been cunning enough herself to have deceived him? Yet surely, however vague he was, he must be aware Mrs Cooper had that soft corner for him. She must over the years have done so many things for him above and beyond her duties that he could not but have noticed. So would he have been able to see that Mrs Cooper might, just, have suddenly acted apparently against his interests in order that he could at last resign and write that book? And, if he had worked this out, what would he do? Even now as he sat in silence, beginning to suck a little at the pipe he had stuck in his mouth, was he starting to work it out? Then would he, seizing on the opportunity she had perhaps attempted to make for him, defend her with whatever lies came into his head?

'Inspector, what you suggest astonishes me. I do not think you can be right.'

The Principal shook his head in bewilderment.

'No, Inspector,' he went on, laying his pipe down beside the rack, 'I cannot believe it. If Mrs Cooper was so disloyal, she would have shown signs of it before. And she has not, not in all the years she has worked for me.'

'I am sorry, sir, that I have had to ask,' he said eventually. 'But you will know an investigating officer has to think of each and every possibility.'

'Yes, yes, Inspector, I quite understand. But I think you can really take my word for it that Mrs Cooper simply would never have done anything so disloyal as to steal an examination question-paper. Oh, no, no.'

And, Ghote thought, he really should take the Principal's word for it. Mrs Cooper was not a suspect.

Or . . . Or was she, despite everything?

The only absolutely definite thing that had emerged from this interview, really, was that the trapping coils round an adage could go on and on winding out.

But could he ask Principal Bembalkar, who, Mrs Cooper had told him, frequently used the phrase about the poor cat, just what 'an adage' was?

No, he could not. He did not see how he possibly could.

'Thank you, sir,' he said, getting to his feet. 'You have been most helpful.'

But that was not at all true.

17

Standing beside Mrs Cooper's desk, Ghote at once put the only question he felt was left to him in the matter of the missing Statistics Techniques paper. Questions about Somnomax Five and the use that had been made of it, however much they were at the forefront of his mind, had to be kept rigorously locked away. Additional Commissioner's orders.

'Please,' he said to the now friendly rakshas, 'I have been thinking very much about the time there was nobody here itself to stop that question-paper being stolen. Can you kindly tell if Principalji had any appointments last Monday just before he was usually taking lunch. You are knowing he went early that day?'

'One moment,' she replied, 'I will look at his book.'

From the drawer in front of her she produced a heavy leather-bound engagement diary. She flipped through its pages.

'Ah, yes, here.'

Ghote felt a flicker of hope. And would not let it flame up too high.

Mrs Cooper read.

'Yes, at that time Principalji had arranged to be seeing Dr Mrs Gulabchand. Proposal to add to Modern Poets course. Thomas Hardy.'

Mrs Gulabchand. Ghote allowed that flame to take a little leap. So one of the people who had access to Somnomax Five, had actually been in this very room, had been here alone, just beside the Principal's door at the time his keys were dangling invitingly in it.

He almost turned that instant and left at a run.

But he had learnt something about adages and the way their coils multiplied and multiplied. Was it going to turn out now as encoilingly as before that, however unlikely it seemed, other people, Professor Kapur, even Victor Furtado, had also had appointments with the Principal at that exact time?

'Please, who else was due to see Principalji then?'

'But no one, Inspector. If Principalji was going to discuss important subject like extension of Modern Poets syllabus he was going to give plenty of time for same.'

'Yes. Yes, I suppose that must be so.'

He had never heard of this Hardy Thomas, Thomas Hardy, but presumably adding the name of some modern poet, possibly a political subversive, to a course was a matter requiring much discussion.

However, the main thing now was that Mrs Gulabchand was the only person who had had any reason to come into this outer office, to see the keys in Principal Bembalkar's chamber door, at that time.

Now he did let hope blaze up.

He hardly thanked Mrs Cooper before yet again he was marching along the veranda outside, clattering down the deserted stairs and hurrying towards the wide open doors. In his haste he just knocked into the blackboard stating that this was a Day of Mourning.

Or, no, he realised just as he was about to step into the sun-blazed open. Someone – probably Dean Potdar himself – had put a new message on the board. He turned back for an instant.

Founder's Day Holiday Cancelled Owing to Day of Mourning All classes will be held as usual on Thursday

Well, that would seem to be fair, he thought, settling the board square on its easel again. Students had had one day without classes. They could not expect another so soon.

He ran out into the compound.

In less than twenty minutes he was ringing the bell of the Gulabchands' flat in the Ramaprakash Housing Society block down at Dhake Colony.

The simpleton servant with the white uniform and golden yellow cummerbund opened the door.

'Mrs Gulabchand? She is inside?'

'Ji haan, sahib.'

'Say, it is Inspector Ghote, Crime Branch.'

The fellow drifted away.

And returned after three long minutes had passed.

'Please come.'

He led Ghote out, once again, to the balcony where the swing with the red plastic seat stood idle and Mrs Gulabchand sat in the wicker armchair that Dean Potdar had occupied while he himself had found the foil sheet of Somnomax Five in the flat's bedroom. She was a lady in full middle age, solidly stout in a plain cream-coloured sari with a dull red border. Her face, which was large and soft, was set in an expression of immovable placidity.

She had been reading, and on a cane stool beside her the pamphlet she had put down lay next to a pair of heavy horn-rim spectacles. Ghote took a quick look at the thin booklet, hoping that whatever it was might give him a further clue to the lady's personality.

All-India Blind Faith Eradication Committee Annual Report.

Yes, that was a clue, surely. The reader of such a report would very likely be determined to get for such views the very maximum influence. And what better position of influence was there for her than to be principal of a college where young men and women formed their ideas? Mrs Gulabchand must very likely have been ready to go to the length of stealing a question-paper in order to get rid of poor Dr Bembalkar.

As ready – the thought struck him like a sudden blow to the stomach – as Professor Kapur almost certainly was for his own altogether different ends.

Another length of tough creeper whipping round to thicken the trap, the adage, the add-age.

Yet Mrs Gulabchand or her husband had had, in that bedside table, Somnomax Five. Damn it, the third foil sheet of the stuff he had taken from it was still in the back pocket of the very trousers he was wearing. There had been nowhere else safe to keep such irregularly obtained evidence.

'Madam,' he began, urging himself with every syllable to be cautious, to remember the Additional Commissioner's order. 'Madam, you are most probably aware that I am investigating the disappearance from the chamber of Principal Bembalkar of one question-paper, Statistical Techniques.'

Mrs Gulabchand slightly inclined her head in acknowledgement.

Ghote was suddenly reminded of the statue of Queen-Empress Victoria he had seen once years ago when he had taken Ved to the Victoria Gardens. There they had regarded for some time the corpulent figure, removed long before from its place of honour in the city to rest, ignored and noseless, but still firm with majesty and unassailable dignity, in a scrubby neglected corner.

'Perhaps you are not aware, however, madam,' he said, 'at what period it was last Monday when that paper was – '

He balked at the word *stolen*. Somehow, in the face of the solid pillar of respectability he had seen Mrs Gulabchand as being, it did not seem right to produce as blunt an expression. Not even if she was, possibly, probably, the thief and in consequence a murderer at least by intention.

' . . . when that paper was removed.'

'You will tell me, Inspector.'

Mrs Gulabchand's voice was calm assurance itself. Could it really be he was interrogating, if in the most roundabout way, someone who had nearly sent to death young Bala Chambhar?

'Madam, it was between 12.30 p.m. and, at latest, 2 p.m.'

'Very well, Inspector.'

Again Mrs Gulabchand inclined her head.

'Madam, I am informed that you yourself had an appointment that day at 12.30 p.m. itself with Principal Bembalkar.'

'And what if I did, Inspector?'

Was that an evasion, the little give-away wrongness he hoped to detect in interrogating any suspect? Even if this placid answer was very different from the sliding away from an inconvenient question he was used to dealing with with riff-raffs like the city's anti-socials. So was he getting nearer?

He went into the attack again. Still with unremitting caution.

'Please, can you kindly tell me what occurred when you went for that appointment?'

For a long moment Mrs Gulabchand did not answer.

What is she doing? What is she thinking, Ghote asked himself. Is she preparing some lie? Is she wondering whether she has been brought suddenly to the point where she must confess? Am I at the end of it all? Have I weaved and wriggled my way out of that damn adage after all?

Then Mrs Gulabchand spoke.

'Inspector, I wonder why you are asking me this? Is it because you have got it into your head that I myself had something to do with that question-paper being taken? Dean Potdar was telling me you believe, for some reason, that the boy Bala Chambhar was not responsible for the actual theft.'

'Yes, madam, that is so. Bala could not have taken the paper itself.'

'Inspector, I asked you a question.'

Once more Ghote swallowed. His throat was dry.

'Madam,' he said, 'it is my duty as investigating officer to ask each and every person who was in the vicinity of Principal's office at the time in question what exactly it was they were doing at the said time.'

'So you are making no accusation?'

There was something triumphant in her voice. Not any loud and noisy triumph for the whole world to hear, but instead a quiet satisfaction. The satisfaction of someone who had got their own way. More, the satisfaction – Ghote felt sure – of someone who was very much used to getting their own way, eventually. Someone who had found in the course of their life that quiet and unyielding persistence served to achieve their ends, time and time again.

'No, madam,' he said, 'I am not at all making any accusation. I am merely hoping to learn if you were seeing any other individual in or near the Principal's office at that hour.'

'Then, Inspector, I am able to say to you that I did not. There were some students below in the courtyard. There had been some jape or disturbance going on. But that was over, and they were departing. But when I found Principal Bembalkar was not present to keep his appointment with me I left.'

'I see. And, madam, were you by chance noticing one thing?'

'Yes, Inspector?'

Mrs Gulabchand was retaining all her solid calm. All Queen-Empress Victoria's solid authority.

'Madam, were you noticing some keys in the door of the Principal's chamber?'

'Yes, Inspector. They were there. It was when I saw them I realised Dr Bembalkar had left. As his secretary was also absent I went to Dean Potdar's office and learnt there that Dr Bembalkar had gone early to his lunch. I was surprised, but there was nothing to do but to leave in my turn.'

She had remained absolutely unmoved while she had spoken, clearly and softly, about the keys.

If instead of looking only, Ghote asked himself, she had turned that key in the lock, had gone into that chamber, had seen the question-papers and had suddenly realised what she could do by taking just one and getting it sold round entire Bombay, would she have been able to keep up such an appearance of calm?

Probably, yes, she would have been capable of that. A woman of that slow and undeviating persistence would tread like a gentle elephant over even such an obstacle.

So he had come up against a wall too high to climb, too thick to break through.

There was nothing else for it but to acknowledge that. If there was evidence against Mrs Gulabchand, there was not a shred of definite proof. The evidence against Professor Kapur was as strong, in fact. The astrologer had as good a reason, exactly as good, as Mrs Gulabchand's for taking advantage of Principal Bembalkar's lapse. He, too, had had access to Somnomax Five. And, if he had not admitted to being at the scene of the theft at the time, he had refused to say where he was.

Even Victor Furtado was not established as impossible, even though he apparently had no Somnomax Five. Someone intelligent enough to have become, despite appearances, a college lecturer surely would have had the sense to have got rid of the evidence of having used sleeping tablets if he had somehow acquired them?

Mrs Gulabchand, if she was lying about that visit to the Principal's office, had had, of course, to keep the remains of her supply because her husband might have asked about the pack had she thrown it away altogether, and Professor Kapur could well have forgotten using, perhaps months before, that strip of foil as a bookmark. Neither had there been anything to prevent Victor Furtado going into Principal Bembalkar's empty outer office after Mrs Gulabchand had left, if it was the simple truth she had been telling. There must have been some time when the question-papers inside remained there for the taking.

So he was no further forward, either in producing a report on the question-paper to be sent to the Centre, or in gathering hard evidence about who had attempted to kill Bala Chambhar.

And, he realised with a new thump of dismay, there was nothing more he could do immediately about getting that report for the Centre. This was Oceanic College's Day of Mourning. He had seen no one about out there except Dean Potdar, Principal Bembalkar and Mrs Cooper. There was, it had been altogether evident, no one else in the whole place to see. Security Officer Amar Nath had not been there. Krishna Iyer MA Madras had not been at his post at the cycle stand. Not a student had been there, not a teacher. There was no one. No one. No one to see. No one to ask. Anything.

18

There was nothing Ghote could do now. His report, already much more delayed than the CBI wallas' one he had hoped to show up, would have to wait at least for another twenty-four hours. If he managed to unravel the business even then.

The only thing left was to go back to Headquarters and get on with any routine work on his desk. But at Headquarters what was more likely than that the Additional Commissioner would ask what progress he had made? And to say in reply that he was at a dead end because of Dean Potdar's cunning notion of declaring a Day of Mourning and emptying Oceanic College would be to put his head right into the tiger's mouth.

Then a thought came to him. A happy idea.

He would not go back to Headquarters. He would go home. He was entitled to take rest. He had been out at the college and fighting his way there and back for many more hours than strict duty laid down. And, besides, there really was nothing he could do till next day.

No, a good rest was what he deserved. And, taking it, he might after all come up with some way of getting to that answer.

He headed for home feeling better than he had done ever since his early morning start. For the rest of the day his way was clear before him, even if it could lead nowhere. He had done all he could.

It was not until, more than an hour later, he arrived home that it struck him that there was something else he could do there besides taking that needed rest. He could beat his wife.

All the circumstances were right. Ved would be at school. Protima would have done her shopping early when there was the best choice in the market. They would have the place to themselves.

Then, abruptly, he was overcome with confusion. He had not planned this out. He had not had time to. To begin with, he had never definitely settled on just what he would use. He remembered that, sitting in the Oceanic College students canteen, he had decided, more or less, that the right thing would be a good leather belt such as some of his fellow officers boasted of using. But he had not got any such thing. Merely three or four cotton or nylon ones plus his best-uniform Sam Browne belt. But to make use of that, even if it would be practical to clutch that brass-fitted combination of belt and shoulder strap, was unthinkable. It was the symbol of his calling as an officer of police.

While he had been waiting for Mohinder Singh Mann he had half-decided on a cane or a whippy stick of some sort. But, again, he had no such thing to hand.

In the meantime, quite without thinking, he had rattled the latch on the door. Now Protima opened it.

'It is you,' she exclaimed, much surprised. 'Are you well? What it is?'

The look of instant concern on her face at once chased away all thoughts of dealing out retribution for past offences.

'No, no,' he said. 'I am quite well. Hundred percent, except only I am damn hot.'

'Come inside, come inside. I will bring you a cold drink. Take off your shoes. Sit, sit.'

He went in and dropped into his chair.

But even as he did so a tiny prickle of resentment ran up and down inside him. Yes, what Protima had suggested was exactly what he wanted. But he had not wanted her to tell him what he wanted. If he had said, 'Fetch me one cold drink. I am going to take off my shoes and take rest', then he would have been delighted to sit, to sip slowly at the cold drink when she brought it. Limca. Limca would be nicest, tart and refreshing.

He bounced angrily to his feet.

'But you are not sitting,' Protima said, coming back with a glass and a bottle of Mangola. 'Sit, sit. Let me take off those shoes. How hot you are looking. Sit and drink this only.'

Now. Now would be the time to do it. Now when she had brought him syrupy Mangola which she obstinately believed he particularly liked because she herself did. Now when she had ordered him to sit rather than waiting for him to sit or stay standing as he liked. Now would be the time to beat her into a different frame of mind. From henceforth only.

Except.

Except what was he to do it with? He looked down at the shoes he had not kicked off. One of them might do, though it was too stiff and clumsy to get a good grip on.

He glanced rapidly round the room. Nothing. No stick of any sort. Nor anything that could at all substitute for a leather belt.

He could march into the bedroom and find one of his chappals there. But he had rejected a chappal as being too childish for the importance he wanted to give to this. Or there was a hairbrush. Her own hairbrush.

But, no. In their early married days they had sometimes played a game of him pretending to spank her with a hairbrush. With the very same hairbrush she still used. To use that would give quite the wrong signal.

Wait, a broom. Surely they had a broom somewhere in the kitchen or just outside. A bundle of straight thin hard twigs would be just right, just the right length, about two feet, just the right whippiness. But. But the broom, if he could remember where it was kept, would be appallingly dirty. It would not be right to use such a thing.

'But still you are not sitting? Are you dreaming only? And still you are looking hot. Hotter even than before. Now, sit at once.'

And he sat.

Protima poured the Mangola, crouched and pulled off his shoes.

Certainly, that felt better. And it was delightful to be sitting. He leant back.

Perhaps later. Later this afternoon. When occasion arose. There was plenty of time before Ved would get back from school.

He drank the Mangola. It was pleasant, and deliciously cold. And if it was more syrupy than he liked, well, it was.

'So, now, tell me,' Protima said, going to put his shoes by the door, 'why have you come home so early? The case? Is it over?'

'Oh, if only it were,' he exclaimed before it occurred to him that he did not really want to have to tell her anything about that terrible adage he was encoiled and entrapped inside.

And in any case talking about the business would mean, if he was not careful, explaining to her what an adage was. And that was something he was totally unable to do. How stupid he would look.

He squeezed his eyes half-shut and tried to picture yet one more time that old, old school notebook. *Adage* = Equals what? The picture, as ever, eluded his inner vision.

'Tell me about it,' Protima said.

'No. No, I do not want.'

'But why not?'

'I just only do not want.'

'But that is nonsense. You know sometimes when a case has been extra difficult you have told me about it, and by the time you had finished you were able to see what you had missed.'

'I was able to see,' he snapped out bitterly. 'You are meaning that Madam Detective solved the case when her poor husband could not.'

But that, in one instance at least, had been true. Or partly true. He felt a searing burn of resentment.

'No, no,' Protima said. 'You know well I am not at all able to do your work. All I was meaning was that sometimes, when you tell me your all problems, you yourself are seeing what is answer.'

And that, again, was true. Absolutely true.

Which did nothing to lessen his feeling of fury.

So, now. Now was the time to teach her that lesson.

No. No, it was somehow too soon. Not the true and proper moment. It would be wrong to let her think what he did was just because of one thing she had said. It all must be done calmly. In the way a magistrate handed down sentence.

So, watching himself like a neck-swivelling vulture in case that word 'adage' slipped out, he started at least to give her the outline of the business that had entangled him in so many twists and turns.

Soon he found he was recounting every last detail. How he had learnt a little about Oceanic College during that absurd night morcha, striding along beside green, swaying, spring-fresh Sarita Karatkar. How he had overcome eventually every obstacle in getting to see Principal Bembalkar. How in that long battle of wills with the Principal he had at last learnt about the keys left to dangle in his chamber door. How he had worked out what the reason for taking just that one question-paper must be, and how he had discovered there were only two candidates for the principalship who could have done what had been done.

Here Protima had interrupted.

'But are you sure there could be no other reason than to make this Principal resign so as to take his seat?'

'Oh yes,' he had answered, irritation seeping upwards again, 'Dean Potdar was suggesting that one Mr Victor Furtado, a young lecturer Principal Bembalkar had failed to rescue from a rag, might have done it out of revenge only.'

Protima had laughed at that.

'Come, you are not in some film. It is not Naseeruddin Shah playing Inspector.'

And, yes, he thought, before he had had time to resent her remark, she is right. It is absurd to think of a man like Victor Furtado attempting to discredit the Principal in that way.

But then Protima had gone on to add something that did bring his resentment, boiling and bubbling, to the surface.

'No,' she had said, 'there really must be some other reason, besides making that Principal resign, for taking away that question-paper.'

'What? What reason. What?' he had shot back. 'Tell me one good reason for anyone to do that. Just only one.'

It would be too bad, altogether too bad, he thought with sharp rattling anger, if Protima finds the answer I have not at all been getting near. How then will I ever be able to act as a husband should? To beat my wife for daring to put her way over mine?

'Well, I am not knowing,' she said then. 'Perhaps you are right.'

'Yes. Yes, I am right. One hundred and one percent right.'

After that he had lapsed into sullen silence. But when at last Protima had said coaxingly 'But go on, tell more. It is a so difficult business,' he had grumblingly complied and explained at great length about the more appalling crime he seemed to have discovered at the KEM Hospital and in that bare little room in Chawl No 4.

For all of that Protima had had nothing but praise and admiration.

Well – the thought just tickled the edge of his mind – perhaps after all she is more of a good Hindu wife than I was believing.

But at once the memory of the choice of Ved's college, even of the insistence on Mangola over Limca, came back to him, and he abandoned his half-fulfilled change of mind.

Before much longer he felt he had been right to do so. It was when he had reached the point in his long narrative, which in the beginning he had not expected to tell, where the Additional Commissioner had given him the order not to take time himself to investigate the possible murder, or attempted murder, of Bala Chambhar.

'But that is not right,' Protima exclaimed. 'No, you must not let that man tell you what you must do. You must investigate that poisoned shrikhand to the very end.'

Then anger rose up in him once more. Full and fiery.

How dare she. How dare she tell him what he must or must not do in his working life. How dare she set herself up against the Additional Commissioner himself.

Yes, she did deserve a sound thrashing. Here and now. With whatever first came to hand. Chappal, broom, hairbrush, even Sam Browne belt itself. Yes. Now.

He jumped up from his chair.

And at the outer door came a noisy, familiar tapping.

Ved. It was Ved back from school.

Like a child's balloon, its tied neck suddenly untwisted, Ghote sank back into his chair.

19

Once more Ghote made sure he arrived at Oceanic College well before the start of classes. He was feeling grey with depression at the prospect in front of him, although he knew this was as much as anything because of the frustrated time he had spent at home, miserable and uneasy. Ved had chosen not to go out, and so he had found he had lost any opportunity for doing what he had been on the point of doing – surely, surely? – when his son had tapped at the door. He had sat there feeling dully furious with Protima, feeling as furious with himself, even feeling furious with Ved for working at his school books instead of begging to be allowed to go and see his friends 'just only for one half-hour'.

But at least now he was determined to have the maximum time to dig and burrow as hard as he could everywhere in the college, however little chance there seemed to be of getting to the heart of the business. There must, he told himself angrily, be someone who had been somewhere near the offices on the balcony during the time the question-paper was stolen. All right, no one might actually have seen some unauthorised person disappear through Mrs Cooper's door. But there ought to be someone, or a succession of people, who had been somewhere in the vicinity and who should remember seeing anyone else there. Perhaps a person who had no good reason to be up on the balcony just then.

Possibly even, if luck was really with him, he would find a student or perhaps a peon carrying a message or a file, who had actually seen Professor Kapur where he had denied ever being. It would be a pleasure to confront that gentleman with a witness to his lying.

He had decided on the way out, going past the factories and mills, smoke creeping oily and black from their chimneys even at this early hour, that he would begin by stationing himself at the cycle stand again. There he would ask every single student he could catch where exactly they had been at around midday on the day of the crime. He might, too, have better luck than he had had before in discovering one of Bala Chambhar's particular friends. They, in turn, might know who it was who had handed Bala the stolen paper. Or perhaps have been told by Bala simply how it was he had come across it, which in itself might be enough of a clue to the original thief.

Unless, he thought with a sudden squirt of bitterness, Protima was somehow right and the question-paper had not after all been stolen as a means of making Principal Bembalkar resign.

He thrust that notion away. Protima could not be right. She must not be right.

At the college compound he saw, with some grudging pleasure, that at least today things were back to normal. Krishna Iyer, MA Madras, was back on duty, at his still empty cycle stand, shunting about here and there, busy and puffed-up, but aimless. The doors of the building were standing wide open and the tall figure of Amar Nath in his green uniform could be seen looking out at the world from just inside, ready to jump on the first of the students as they made their way in. And only three or four minutes after his own arrival the earliest students did begin to put in an appearance.

But, though he succeeded in getting hold of as many as twenty or even twenty-five boys and a little later a dozen or so girls, and after that a number of peons and even a couple of sweepers, he got nowhere. The theft of the question-paper had taken place during the lunch recess. So it was natural that almost everybody in the college, students, staff, peons, everyone, was eating the midday meal. The staff had almost all been in their common room, where lunch was served. The students had crowded into the canteen or risked the over-boiled tea and greasy omelets of the Paris Hotel, or those of them with well-off parents had gone to the cars that had come from home carrying food, home-cooked in best ghee, in steel containers. Peons and sweepers had crouched where they could, chewing at what they had.

Nor did any of the students he spoke to admit to knowing Bala Chambhar more than by sight. Again, he thought, that was reasonable. From all that Sarita and Mohinder Singh Mann had told him Bala was something of a loner. So if in his questioning now he had not chanced to come on one of his few friends, or even someone who knew who they were, this was not out of the way.

In the end, when the students were in the first classes and the compound deserted, he thought he would have to bring himself to undergo yet another consultation with Dean Potdar. It would risk his being accompanied for the rest of the day by a Dr Watson who totally reversed the standard relationship between Great Detective and humble hanger-on. But that was a penalty that would have to be paid.

So eventually, having wandered about for some time hoping to catch one or two more students for some reason not in their classes, again he made his way gloomily up the stairs to the balcony.

Then, just as he was passing Mrs Cooper's door, an extraordinary figure shot out of the Dean's office ahead. It was his secretary, the comfortable knitter. But she looked anything but comfortable now. Her face was a picture of shock, mouth stuck half open, eyes rolling upwards. In her hand she still clutched the piece of knitting she had been working at. It trailed at her side, unravelling more and more with every lunging step.

'Inspector, Inspector,' she managed to gasp out. 'Help. Help.'

What has happened now in this crazy place, he thought with a jab of viciousness.

For half a second a vision of pompous, dignified, tubby little Dean Potdar attempting rape flashed into his mind.

But he had no time for speculation.

He strode up to the distraught secretary, grasped her firmly by the arm trailing her knitting, and almost shouted her into coherence.

'Madam. Madam. What is it? What has happened?'

'Dean sahib, Dean sahib,' she moaned, now almost collapsing. 'They have kidnapped him.'

'Kidnapped? What are you meaning, kidnapped?'

'It is true, Inspector. True. Dean sahib seemed to be late this morning, and I was wondering where he could be. Then – then the telephone was ringing. I thought it might be himself. He was perhaps once more indisposed, another of his bad nights. But it was some boys, some boys from the college. We have kidnapped the Dean, one of them was saying. When we are getting our Founder's Day holiday back we would let him go.'

'You recognised the voice? Did whoever it was give a name only?'

'No, no, Inspector. Just that message, and then he was shutting the line. Inspector, you must help. You must save him before they are doing him some injury.'

'Well, madam, this is a matter for local police itself. What you must do is inform Principal Bembalkar, and he will get in touch with your nearest PS.'

Thank goodness, he thought to himself as he took his hand off the secretary's arm, here is something I do not have to deal with. One twisting line of the adage has missed me altogether.

'But, Inspector, you are not understanding. Dean sahib is not at all a hale and hearty man. If they are rough with him, he may be having one heart failure.'

No, oh, no.

If one flicking adage length of fish-line, thorn, pliant bamboo, whatever it was, had seemed to curl round in the wrong direction, it was only so that now another could come in more tightly from the other side.

He gave a huge sigh.

'Very well,' he said, 'I will come with you to the Principal, and then we would see what I can do.'

Together they entered the Principal's office, and, without a word to Mrs Cooper, the Dean's secretary made a stumbling rush to the chamber door and flung it open.

Principal Bembalkar was at his desk, tweed jacket buttoned over sturdy stomach, first pipe of the day sending up a cloud of fragrant blue smoke, heavy-rimmed spectacles focussed on a copy – Ghote took in – of the works of William Shakespeare.

Quickly Ghote explained the situation.

'And, sir,' he concluded, 'I understand from this lady that the Dean could have some heart attack if he is too much shocked. So there is a need to act quickly.'

'Yes,' Principal Bembalkar said in a voice much more remote than Ghote would have liked. 'Yes, something must be done.'

His eyes, however, flicked downwards to the book in front of him. Ghote, following his gaze not without impatience, saw that the play it was opened at was *Hamlet*.

'Sir,' he said, 'you must telephone your local police just now, even if I am able to start some investigations myself.'

'But the police,' Principal Bembalkar said. 'What will it do to the good name of the college if they come here? What more will it do after what has been done already? And Mrs Rajwani, what will she say?'

'Sir, you are having no alternative. You cannot let your students kidnap a senior on your staff and not take all possible action. Sir, you must do it now.'

'Yes,' Dr Bembalkar said with a sigh. 'You are right, of course. Can you . . . Please, Inspector, will you ask Mrs Cooper to telephone and inform the local police of what has happened.'

'Very well, sir.'

'And, Inspector . . .'

'Yes, sir?'

'Should she also make an announcement that the Founder's Day holiday is restored?'

Ghote felt a jolt of water-pure anger.

Why was the fellow asking for his advice? Why could he not make up his mind one way or another, and act? And how could he contemplate giving in to these people, these students, who had gone so far as to kidnap their own Dean?

'Sir,' he shot out. 'That is one hundred percent up to you. But if you are wanting my opinion it would be altogether wrong to give in.'

'Very well. Very well, Inspector. But please do your utmost to find poor Potdar and release him. Before . . . Before anything too appalling happens.'

'Yes, sir,' Ghote said.

But outside, after he had given Mrs Cooper the Principal's message, he wondered what there was he could do. He knew scarcely anything of the college, of who was likely among its several hundred students to do anything so outrageous as this.

Then a thought struck him.

He did know two students, and one a student leader at that. Was it possible that young Mohinder Singh Mann, full of idealism and energy though he undoubtedly was, could have arranged this business? And Sarita Karatkar, that green swaying creature of spring, was she his accomplice? Was it to find details of the kidnapping plan that someone – But who? And why? – had made that attempt to break in to the Student Union office that Sarita had laughingly spoken about?

He glanced at his watch. Nearly 8.30. The first classes would be over in a few minutes, and then, if what Krishna Iyer MA Madras had told him held good for every day, Mohinder and Sarita would go to the canteen.

He hurried down.

The place was still deserted when he arrived, though the tea-urn was steaming gently and the attendant was already behind the counter. But scarcely had he taken this in when, from behind, he heard the stampeding feet of the first students.

Mohinder and Sarita were among them.

He went quickly over, caught hold of the boy by the arm and without a word pushed him back through the hurrying, chattering mass of oncoming students, round to the first quiet spot he could find. Sarita, he realised with mixed feelings, had followed.

'Now,' he said as soon as he had got the tall young Sikh backed up against the slogan-covered wall behind him. 'Now, I want no back answers. I want nothing of shilly-shally. Where is Dean Potdar? Come, answer. Answer or you would find yourself in hundred percent troubles.'

The boy did not understand him.

Or, he said to himself, has he guessed why he has been marched away out of the canteen? And has he – he is quick enough and clever enough – made up his mind to act the complete innocent?

But there was someone who, every bit as quick and clever, was incapable, he felt certain, of such dissimulation.

He put a hand flat on Mohinder's chest to keep him where he was, jerked round and shot out a question at Sarita.

'Now, what are you knowing about this? Quick, tell me. Or it would be the worse for this young man.'

All the sparkling impudence, the impudence he had so much liked despite himself, had left her face. Yes, he had her well and truly frightened.

'Well?' he barked out.

'Inspector . . . Inspector, honestly I don't know – We don't know what you are talking about. It is Dean Potdar? You are asking where he is? But he is in his office. Or, if he is not, where should he be?'

'Where this young man and his fellow riff-raffs have hidden him,' Ghote snarled.

'Hidden – But, no, Inspector, no.'

Mohinder had brought out the words in a manner so troubled and bewildered that Ghote asked himself once more whether the boy could possibly be play-acting. He could have sworn not. Yet, if Mohinder, student leader, was behind the kidnapping, then would this not be the only card he could play?

He turned back to Sarita.

If he was going to break either of them, then she was the one who would snap. However much it hurt him to do it to her.

'Now, you must be knowing also. All right, your friend here was kidnapping the Dean and hoping to get back that Founder's Day holiday. It was one stupid idea. But forget that. Tell me, now only, where the Dean is being kept, and perhaps your Mohinder would not hear any more about it.'

But Sarita's pretty face still retained its look of incomprehension. Was she as cunning as the boy?

'Inspector,' she said, a wonderfully earnest frown appearing on her forehead, 'are you saying someone has kidnapped Dean Potdar? To force the authorities to restore that holiday? But that is nonsense. Nonsense only.'

'Then why did this young man, or one of his friends, telephone the Dean's secretary and make just only that demand? Come, you are trying to fool me. One more chance. I am giving one more chance itself.'

Mohinder, still pinned to the wall, broke in.

'Inspector, what can we say to convince you? Truly, when you were telling us, it was the first we had heard of such an idea. And, I agree, it is damn silly. All right, it was harsh to cancel the holiday when the Day of Mourning had been given with no warning. But to kidnap Old Pot-belly – I mean, Dean Potdar, that is not at all the right way to protest.'

'No,' Sarita broke in. 'It is worse than being just only the wrong way to protest, Mohinderji. It is wrong in itself. Everyone is knowing Pot-belly is not in good health. To kidnap him is wrong. Altogether wrong.'

'Yes,' Mohinder said. 'The most we were thinking of was a dharna. And that would have been at Princi's door not Potdar's.'

'A dharna,' Ghote pounced in. 'You were making protest plans then? You were going to crowd Principal Bembalkar's door, stop each and every coming and going until he was giving in? Now, kindly do not try to tell me you did not in the end decide to go further and hold the Dean to ransom.'

'But we did not,' Mohinder answered, his beardless face beneath his neat turban breaking into a sweat of hot denial. 'We did not, Inspector.'

'Inspector,' Sarita came in from the other side. 'Even if Mohinder had had such a bad idea, I would not have let him do it. We knew Old Pot-belly could collapse at any moment. One heart attack he had had already. I could not have let anyone do that to him.'

And that convinced Ghote.

The passion the girl had put into every syllable of her denial was too simple, too innocent to be anything other than an outpouring of truth.

'Very well,' he said, 'I am believing you. You were not responsible for the kidnapping. But then who is? That you must be able to guess.'

In the quick glance exchanged between the two of them, as quickly hidden, Ghote realised that once they had begun to think about it they each of them knew who must be responsible for what had been done to his plump, twinkling-eyed, malicious Dr Watson.

He fixed Mohinder with an unblinking gaze.

'All right,' he said, 'now you will tell me who those irresponsible boys are.'

'Inspector, I cannot.'

'Will not. Will not is what you are meaning. And I will not put up with that. I can charge you as accessory to the crime, and unless I get those names now, ek dum I would do it.'

'No, Inspector. I refuse to answer.'

'No!'

It was Sarita, explosively breaking in.

'No, Mohinder,' she went on, a little more calmly. 'It is all very well to be loyal. But this is serious. Dean Potdar could die. You know that. Tell the inspector who it is.'

Mohinder's answer hung in the balance. But not for long. Ghote could see that Sarita's arrow-straight glance was too full of passionate fire for the boy to be able to resist.

He turned back to Ghote.

'There must be six–seven of them,' he said. 'They are trouble-makers always. Rich boys. We were thinking of necking them out of the union.'

'And the names?' Ghote persisted.

'It is one Shantaram Antrolikar who is the leader,' Mohinder answered promptly. 'The others, toughs though they are also, are nothing to him.'

'Very well. Now, where can I find this fellow?'

Mohinder thought for a moment.

'That is more difficult,' he said. 'If he has kidnapped the Dean, he must be wherever he is hiding him. And that would not be anywhere easy to find.'

A thought came to Ghote.

'Tell me,' he said, 'was it this Shantaram Antrolikar who was attempting to break into your Union office? Could that be linked somehow to his plan to hide the Dean?'

'No, no,' Mohinder answered at once. 'We have found out who that was.'

Sarita unexpectedly burst into a fit of giggles, biting her under-lip in an attempt to check them.

'Someone actually saw him,' she spluttered. 'It was so funny. He couldn't force the window. Not however much he puffed and panted.'

'Yes,' said Mohinder, grinning himself. 'Just yesterday they were telling us.'

'But who was it?' Ghote asked with mounting fury, still feeling obscurely that the attempted break-in and the kidnapping must somehow be connected.

'It was the great Professor, so-called, Kapur,' Sarita answered, overcoming the last of her giggles. 'We think he wanted to find some evidence to get Mohinder rusticated. Mohinder used to go to his lectures and was asking some very disrespectful questions.'

Professor Kapur, Ghote thought. So he had been doing that at the time the question-paper was taken. No wonder he had refused to say where he had been. Then was he no longer a suspect?

But no time to consider the implications of that now.

'Listen,' Sarita had said with a sudden sharp bounce of discovery, 'Shantaram is accountancy student, yes?'

'Yes, yes,' Mohinder almost shouted in reply.

He turned to Ghote.

'There is an exam in accountancy today,' he said. 'This morning itself, postponed from earlier. Some of our friends are writing it. One hundred percent important.'

'So Shantaram will be in there now,' Sarita concluded in triumph.

'Right,' Ghote said. 'Are you knowing where this is taking place?'

'Yes, here itself,' Sarita answered. 'There was some administrative mess, and they are having to hold it here instead of at the exam centre allocated.'

Ghote felt that luck was suddenly running his way. Twisty thorn-length after twisty thorn-length of the adage whipping away.

'Quick then,' he said. 'Take me there. Take me there, and then we would see some result.'

Led by the two youngsters, at breakneck speed, they hurried along the college's tall corridors, the slogans and crude drawings on the walls flashing by. In less than a minute the two of them pointed to a closed door. On it hung a notice.

Exam in Progress   No Entry   Pin-drop Silence Please Have Respect.

20

Ghote had intended, bursting into the hall where Shantaram Antrolikar ought to be, to go straight up to the invigilator, careless of what disturbance he might be creating, and demand which of the examinees on his list of seat numbers was the boy he wanted. Then he would hustle Antrolikar out as rapidly as he could and deal with him at whatever nearest place was convenient.

His entrance, however, caused no disturbance whatever. A yet greater commotion was already in progress. Victor Furtado, who apparently was the invigilator, must in the course of patrolling the aisles between the rows of tables have come upon some irregularity. But, instead of dealing with it by a whispered word and a stern finger pointing to the door, he had got caught up in a ferocious slanging match.

'No,' the student he confronted was shouting at the moment Ghote had flung the door open. 'No, no, no. I was not at all cheating. I would not. I am not one of those who has paid you Rupees 20 to look all the time at a guide book.'

'How dare you,' Victor Furtado shouted back. 'That is one damn lie. Who has said I have taken money for that?'

All over the hall the other examinees were looking across at the scene with excited interest. Only four or five of the girls made loudly pious shushing sounds and ostentatiously went back to filling up their answer-books.

'Yes, I am daring,' the boy Victor Furtado had challenged yelled back, his face darkening with rage. 'Almost each and every one here has paid you. It is all well known. And those who have not paid are passing notes back and forth as if they were love letters only.'

'Where? Where?' Victor Furtado demanded. 'Show me one boy or girl who has passed a single note.'

Ghote, in fact, could have shown him one then and there, since his eye had fallen on two girls who had taken advantage of the disturbance to exchange information.

'Why should I do your work for you?' the enraged student shot back now. 'And I, I have not paid you. I despise to do it. All I was asking was why this paper I am meant to be answering is containing three-four ridiculous misprints?'

'It is not,' Victor Furtado shouted back, though how he could have known was something that defeated Ghote.

'It is not, it is not, it is not,' Victor Furtado banged on, his nerves plainly altogether breaking down.

But now a student in the next row suddenly came to the Goan lecturer's rescue. He had leapt to his feet, sending his tubing-and-canvas chair sprawling.

'Yes, you are right, Furtadoji,' he shouted. 'That fellow Chauhan is a black-faced cheat. Under his table there are chits containing material relating to subject of examination.'

'That is one damn lie,' the boy Chauhan shouted back.

Even Victor Furtado looked surprised at the accusation. But he bent quickly to look and see whether there were information sheets pinned or pasted under the table.

This was too much for the accused boy, whom Ghote had begun to believe was one of the few in the hall who would not need to pay to be allowed to cheat. Approaching the storm centre, he had noticed how the answer-book on the boy's table was already almost full.

Seeing the lecturer's presented rump now, Chauhan, exasperated, aimed at it a kick with his knee. It cannot, constricted as it was, have hurt and it did not even send Victor Furtado flying. But it did have the effect of overturning Chauhan's own table. Plus setting up opposing choruses of shouts in favour or against.

How long the fracas would have gone on and whether it would have ended in full-out fighting was never to be known. From the dais at the end of the hall there came now a sudden thunderclap of sound that in an instant stilled all the shouts.

Looking round, Ghote saw, standing there holding a spare, folded-up table that had just been battered down on to the invigilator's desk with a single booming reverberation, none other than Professor Kapur, bullet-headed and ferocious.

'That is enough,' the astrologer thundered now. 'Sit down each and every one of you. I will report this, and it will be up to the authorities whether the whole exam is cancelled.'

In half a minute pens and ballpoints were scratching and scribbling once more over the blank pages of the answer-books. Chauhan, giving Victor Furtado one last glare, righted his table, recovered his answer-book and the question-paper with the 'ridiculous misprints' in it and set to again writing furiously.

'Mr Furtado,' Professor Kapur said in ominously quiet tones, 'kindly resume your seat.'

He said no more, but turned and strode from the hall.

Ghote could not prevent a feeling of admiration seeping into his mind. Teacher of astrology Professor Kapur might be, but he was a man of stunning determination too.

However, he had a more pressing matter on his hands.

Quickly he followed Victor Furtado up to the dais. As soon as the Goan had seated himself, he asked him sharply for the number of Shantaram Antrolikar's place.

Victor Furtado, doubtless bemused from the events that had erupted all around him, did not question this sudden demand.

'Yes, yes,' he whispered hurriedly.

It took him, however, several minutes of shuffling back and forth among the lists of nearly a hundred examinees before he looked up at Ghote and whispered 'Seat 73'.

Ghote walked rapidly back through the lines of now assiduously writing students, counting seats as he went.

It did not take him long to reach Seat 73.

He bent down to the boy writing there, only surprised that he did not look particularly big or tough. He had expected, from what Mohinder had said, that Shantaram Antrolikar would be some sort of hulking bully. However, he seemed to be no more than average height and was also wearing a pair of studious-looking spectacles. He was, too, perhaps even more subdued than the examinees around him, some of whom were already once more abandoning their answer-books to take in this new interruption.

'Come with me,' Ghote said into the boy's ear, however. 'Inspector Ghote, Crime Branch, I am wanting one word.'

The boy looked up. His face took on, instant by instant, the appearance of blotted-out fright.

Not such a goonda after all, Ghote thought. I would not have too much of trouble in finding where he has hidden Dean Potdar.

But, despite the boy's appearance of submissiveness, he took care to get a good grip on the elbow of his right arm as he propelled him through the ranks of tables – heads looked up, pens ceased to scratch – and out through the still open door.

In the corridor he saw Mohinder and Sarita waiting. They both started forward.

With a snapped-out 'No' he brushed past and hurried his prisoner away. Luckily catching sight of a classroom apparently unoccupied, he pushed his captive inside and slammed its door closed with his heel.

'Now, Shantaram Antrolikar,' he said. 'I am wanting no nonsense. I know it is you who has kidnapped Dean Potdar, and you are going to tell me straightaway, ek dum, where you have hidden.'

'But – But – '

'I have warned you. You answer now, or you find yourself in one police cell, and there we would not worry too much about how we are getting our informations.'

Behind the boy's large spectacles, already slipping down his nose from the sweat that had started up all over his face, his eyes were wide and fearful. And utterly perplexed.

'But – But – My name is not Shantaram Antrolikar.'

'Now do not try that sort of trick with me. I had your seat number. You were at that table. Very last warning. Where have you got Dean Potdar?'

'But – But, Inspector, there was one only mistake. Two of us were allocated Seat 73. Shantaram was moving. He was saying better to sit next to genius Ram Amelkar than me only.'

At once Ghote knew that this boy, whatever his name was, had been telling the truth. It all fell into place. The boy had not seemed at all like the person Mohinder had described, and both he and Sarita had looked astonished when he had marched this fellow past them.

He turned on his heel and ran from the room.

What if that goonda Antrolikar had noticed what was happening at the seat allocated to him? Would he have guessed why the boy had been taken out? And have slipped away himself, regardless of whether he wrote the exam or not?

Neither Sarita nor Mohinder was to be seen outside the hall now. But he would damn well make sure, if he still could, that he had Antrolikar under his grasp this time, with or without their confirmation.

He paused an instant at the door of the hall – *Pin-drop Silence Please Have Respect* – then, silently as he could so as not to attract his quarry's attention, if the boy was still sitting at his table, he pushed the door open and slipped in.

All inside was quiet. Or comparatively so. Victor Furtado, up on the dais, was looking vaguely ahead into the distance. Below, at more than one spot students leant towards each other once again exchanging whispered information.

Ghote walked quickly and quietly up to Victor Furtado. He took a long look round at the rows of tables, the bent black heads, the coloured shirts of the boys, the bright saris of the girls.

And, to his delight, the only table he saw vacant was at Seat 73.

So Shantaram Antrolikar must still be in the room. Either he had not realised what it meant when the other boy had been marched from the hall, or he had felt himself so secure he was brazening it out. Well, in a minute he would find just how secure he was.

In a rapid undertone he explained to the Goan lecturer what had gone wrong.

'Kindly check through your list of numbers and find which is missing,' he said. 'That must be where Antrolikar is now sitting.'

He endeavoured, while Victor Furtado turned the pages of his long list – why did the fellow have to make such a damn rustling noise? – to efface himself as much as possible.

Could he by thinking hard of something else, anything else, actually become less noticeable? But what to think about? What to find that was not something to do with that bloody adage he was now even more caught up in?

Home. Home life. Ved getting the captaincy of the Regals. Protima.

Oh, yes, it was high time to give Protima more of thought. Ridiculous that he had still not done what he had to do. He had made up his mind, after all. He had made up his mind – the thought occurred to him as somehow significant – just before he had been ordered to investigate all this adage–wrapping business out here. So why had he done nothing? But he had hardly been at home . . . No, see the truth, he had been there yesterday afternoon. What had there really been then to stop him seizing a –

Victor Furtado was whispering urgently.

'Yes? Yes?'

'Antrolikar is in Seat 84. Definitely.'

Looking down, Ghote rapidly worked out from the position of the one unoccupied table, No 73, where No 84 must be. And, yes, the boy looking sullenly at his question-paper there and not writing at all had just the appearance he had expected of Shantaram Antrolikar. He was a hulk of a young man, wearing a shirt of a more vibrant check than any around, with a thick gold chain prominent at his neck, dark-faced and ugly.

Quietly he stepped off the dais and, hoping to be taken for some extra invigilator, set off on a roundabout route so as to approach Antrolikar from the rear.

Only as he got near did he see what had been laid with ostentatious care at the front of the hulking young fellow's table. A knife. A long knife of the sort used by butchers to kill goats.

Oh, yes, he thought, warning to poor Victor Furtado not to try to stop him cheating.

But it was not a question of stopping cheating now. It was something a great deal more serious.

He stepped silently up, leant forward and clamped the long knife hard to the table while with his other hand he fastened a fierce grip on Antrolikar's shoulder.

Then he spoke again the words he had murmured before.

'Inspector Ghote, Crime Branch. You are coming with me.'

And at once he hauled Antrolikar to his feet.

The boy turned, face swelling with dark anger.

But after one moment of doubt he looked away and allowed himself to be led off.

Outside in the corridor the boy from Seat 73 was standing, pale-faced.

'Go back in, go back in,' Ghote snapped. 'And good luck also.'

Then, regardless of the request for pin-drop silence, he pushed Antrolikar hard up against the nearest wall.

'You have kidnapped the Dean of this college,' he said, putting all the implacability he could into his voice. 'You or your friends are keeping him somewhere. Now, where? Where?'

'Go to hell.'

Crack.

Ghote landed a flat-palmed blow on the side of the boy's head. It would, he knew, do him little real harm. But it would damn well hurt.

He hoped, in fact, it would hurt so much that the boy would attempt to respond. Then he could give him something that would really make him think.

But the boy only stood there, looking obstinate.

Ghote gave a long theatrical sigh.

'So you are going to play at being one big-big goonda, is it?' he said.

'Then let me be telling you something. What I am going to do now is to take you to the nearest chowkey and have you locked up.'

'I won't care.'

'No, I do not think you will. But I think you will care for what I would do next.'

'You try your police brutalities on me, and I would see you are in big trouble. My father is one high-up in Rajwani Chemicals.'

Ghote smiled then.

It was a smile he had been reserving to use since this impromptu interrogation had begun, a smile of evident pleasure. But what Shantaram Antrolikar had just said would make it, he hoped, all the more effective when its meaning finally sank in.

'Very good,' he said. 'Now what is this father of yours going to say when he is hearing I have not touched one hair of your head, but that I have gone to Principal Bembalkar and made sure he will boot you out, no BA, no nice label to get a fine job after?'

It took the boy a second or two to grasp it. Ghote could see on his face when it had happened. A sudden look of baffled fury.

'Listen,' the boy said at last. 'Keeping Old Pot-belly out of the way one – two hours, one – two days even, that is just only one good joke.'

'And when he is having heart attack? You are damn well knowing he has heart condition. Every one in your damn college is knowing. So, when he has that, where are you going to laugh at your good joke then?'

'But – But why should he do that?' the boy protested, his voice rising to a surprising whine. 'He would not die. He would not.'

'Now,' Ghote snapped out, 'where are your friends keeping him?'

Another moment of baffled longing not to be where he was.

'At the back of Paris Hotel. That fellow there is one good friend to us.'

'Then you had better go back to your seat and see if you can write one correct answer. If I am finding the Dean, and if he is still in good health, then I will have a word with Mr Furtado and you would not have been outside during whole course of exam.'

'Yes. Yes. All right. I am going.'

The boy positively scuttled away. It did Ghote, watching to make sure he actually went back in, some good to see him. Perhaps now, despite all past disappointments, the coiling adage was beginning to break apart.

But, just at the door of the hall Antrolikar turned and called out.

'Inspector, get plenty of police if you go there. Those fellows are ready to fight, and none of them would worry about not getting BA.'

Then he quickly opened the door and slipped in.

Ghote stood for longer than he had meant to, thinking.

Perhaps young Antrolikar had proved to be less tough than Mohinder had believed. He had had a weakness, and it had been something to use against him. But it looked as if his friends at the Paris Hotel were going to be different. If they really were prepared to fight to keep the Dean hostage it was not going to be easy to rescue the fat little man without those 'plenty of police'.

But for how much longer was it safe to leave the explosive academic in the hands of his tormentors? And how much longer could he himself afford to spend time over it? Damn it, he was here to find out, as quickly as possible on orders from Delhi, how that question-paper had been stolen. And Bala Chambhar, there was him too. Lying in that coma. Or perhaps dead now. Murdered.

Yet Dean Potdar might break out in a fatal rage at any moment. From what he himself had learnt about him in those humiliating sessions trying to use him to find out about the college he had shown every sign of resenting anyone attempting to tell him what he could do. He would resent it even more if it was some students bossing him. So the chances really were high that a heart attack could come at any minute. He could not leave him there at death's door.

But to arrange to have the Paris Hotel surrounded by police and then to raid it might take hours.

Best to try and tackle the place on his own? At once? Yes.

Yes.

More lines tricking and entangling round that damn adage.

21

Setting out for the Paris Hotel, Ghote found himself impelled to hurry and at the same time leadenly inclined to delay. He was all too conscious of the need to rescue tubby, heart-attack prone Dean Potdar with maximum speed. But he was equally very much aware that effecting a rescue single-handedly might well be a straight path to disaster.

Turning the corner into the entrance hall, he saw the lanky figure of Amar Nath. In a jump of decision he made up his mind to recruit him.

The fellow, for all his rough-and-ready approach, was quick enough to take in the situation.

'By God,' he said as soon as Ghote had outlined it, 'they have dared to kidnap Potdar sahib, is it? Oh, I would like to be there when he is shelling those fellows. He would give them plenty mustard.'

He gave a roar of laughter.

'Oh, yes,' he went on. 'So much of mustard, and then – Then, poof. You are knowing that little fatty has got one bad heart?'

'Yes,' Ghote said.

'So we must be getting him back, one, two, three, no? If he is not already lying dead mutton at those fellows' feet.'

'So, chalo,' Ghote said urgently.

Striding along beside the security man, it was all Ghote could do to keep up. And already he was beginning to suspect that taking the fellow along might not have been such a good idea.

'Listen,' he said, making an effort not to gasp a little from the speed of their progress across the compound. 'Listen, when we are getting there it will be a matter of making one careful approach. I want to do this without any whiff of troubles. So take your time from me, no?'

'Oh, yes, yes,' Amar Nath responded. 'Just what you like, Inspectorji.'

Although the words were an acknowledgement, Ghote felt that their cheerful tone hardly echoed it. But he had enlisted the fellow now, and in any case if he met any opposition he was likely to need every bit of muscle to be had.

Ought he to have risked the delay and waited till he had a squad of tough constables ready to go in? But the decision had been taken now. And – he thought of Amar Nath's crude 'poof' – surely it was the right one.

They crossed the road towards the Paris Hotel. Amar Nath seemed determined to be first to get there. Ghote, without quite actually running, contrived just to outpace him.

Looking in from outside, the place seemed no different from the two other occasions he had been there, on that first morning with Amar Nath and when he had just poked his head inside as he had waited till Mohinder Singh Mann would get to the student canteen. Not the least sign of any unusual activity.

The oily proprietor was sitting just as he had been before, poring over his stained and spotted account book. The same out-of-date calendars hung at the same slight angles on the blue peeling walls. The same boy was mopping listlessly as ever at one of the tables. The smell of over-boiled tea still pervaded everywhere.

Was it ever made fresh?

But he had no time to attempt to work out an answer to that.

In the gloom at the back of the place he made out now four hefty young men clustered round a game of cards at a table just beside the doorway into the kitchen. None of them looked exactly unlike a student. But there was something about them, something in the insolent set of their shoulders, in the way their shirts were all unbuttoned to the waist, that, despite the glimpses to be had of well-off young men's thick wristwatches, jewel-glinting rings and heavy gold neck chains, said to Ghote one word: goondas.

Yes, he thought, I have seen types much like these in the slums, hanging around the door of some crime boss, young men ready at his one command to beat up anyone he points at. Or anyone just only taking their fancy. These fellows here may be educated, but they are not one bit different from slum riff-raffs.

He had intended to take a seat at one of the far tables, casually order tea and, after a while when nobody was taking notice, slip into the kitchen. Leaving Amar Nath behind if possible, he would then see what he could find. But he realised now this was impossible. Although the group at the table seemed engrossed in their game of rummy, slapping the cards down with boasting shouts and roars of laughter, it was evident enough they were sitting where they were to make sure nobody except the tea boy went through the doorway beside them.

So what to do? Settle down at a table near the front of the place, order tea – no doubt Amar Nath would want toast, an omelet – and to see what would happen. That seemed best.

But before he had time to turn to the proprietor any decision was taken out of his hands.

With a single great battle shout, Amar Nath simply charged straight at the group at the far end.

He might have brought it off. They had barely turned from their game when he was on them. Their table crashed to the floor. Two of them fell with it. Ghote, standing momentarily transfixed, saw a third take a fearsome punch to the face that clearly put him out of things.

But the odds were such that even the tall Punjabi could not win at. In a moment the one he had not accounted for was hurling himself on to him. With a thunderous jar he fell to the floor. Now, the first two were up again and plunging forward. In the heap of struggling bodies – another table went spinning – fists rose and fell.

Ghote had darted forward, cursing Amar Nath for ruining what chance they had of getting the Dean out alive. Even with the two of them fighting full out there was now little hope of getting the better of these young brutes.

But then he had halted.

No knives were in evidence. Nor any other weapons. And, however overwhelmed Amar Nath was, his opponents were too closely pressed down on him for any of them, even the first fellow now hovering to plant kicks, to do serious damage.

So, taking a moment to mark out his path, he ran lightly forward, swerved past the tangle of threshing limbs, jumped clear over the body of the boy Amar Nath had knocked out and an instant later was through the doorway into the kitchen.

There he saw an elderly nut-faced man with one long protruding yellow tooth, bare to the waist, evidently the cook. No trouble from him. And, of course, no sign of Dean Potdar.

But there was a door at the far end, standing open for coolness.

He ran towards it, darted through and found he had come into a little cramped high-walled compound, cluttered with rubbish of all sorts, empty cold-drink crates, half-squashed cartons, plastic canisters. But in a corner there was a small shelter or large cupboard made out of thick, tar-spattered planks. It had a door, of sorts, with a big, grey padlock dangling down from it.

There. If Dean Potdar was anywhere he must be in there.

He looked furiously all round. And could see nothing he could use to lever the hasp of the padlock away.

Where would the key be? Easy answer. In the pocket of one of those young anti-socials even now thumping at Amar Nath. And before too long they would have finished with that idiot, and then they would realise where it was that he himself had gone. And would come for him.

In despair he went up to the shed door and tugged at the padlock with his bare hands.

It had not been snapped to. The whole thing slipped clear as if it had been a simple hook hanging from the hasp.

He hauled the thick door open.

They had tied Dean Potdar up. He was slumped in the dark in a corner of the narrow shelter, rope wound round and round his tubby frame. His pince-nez had disappeared. His chubby face was dark with suffused blood. His necktie had been taken off and jammed deeply into his mouth and knotted at the back of his head. But in the light from the opened door it was plain to see his little piggy eyes were glittering with life.

What to do for him? Without a knife, it would take minutes at the least to get rid of those ropes. And minutes, in all likelihood, were what he did not have.

He bent towards the bundled figure, put his arms round him and tugged him upright. Twirling and twisting him then like some sort of barrel, he managed to get him into the full daylight.

But there was no way out of the compound except back through the kitchen and the chaikhana itself.

From inside he could hear shouts. Of triumph? Of continuing battle?

He looked round distractedly.

No, there was only one thing for it. The wall at the back was high, but perhaps not too high. It would be dangerous to heave a man with a weak heart over it. But not as dangerous as to wait where they were.

He stooped, changed his grip on the bundle that the Dean was and lifted. The little fat man was almost too heavy for him, but he managed to stagger the few feet across to the wall.

And there, with one enormous effort, he lifted his burden up as high as he could and tumbled it, him, over.

He looked round again, grabbed two cold-drink crates, set one on top of the other, climbed on to them and, as they swayed and rocked, succeeded in flinging himself up on to the top of the wall. Lying flat there, he swung himself round on his stomach and let himself tumble down on the far side.

For a moment he lay breathless, sick and exhausted on the ground where he had fallen, just aware that beside him the Dean was also lying, a dusty and battered bale.

Then he stirred himself.

If he had been able to get over the wall, those young men, when they had finally dealt with Amar Nath, would not have much difficulty following. And they might well still think it worth their while.

He forced himself up on to his knees, swivelled round towards his former Dr Watson and began to tackle the ropes tightly binding him.

Luck seemed to be on his side. The first knot he tugged at yielded easily, and, with it loosened, all the rope fell clear. He heaved the Dean to his feet and stood for a moment looking at him. Though still gagged and too cramped to be able to do more than take a staggering step or two, the little man appeared not to be too much affected by his experiences. His eyes, indeed, were blazing like two tiny hot headlights.

'Dean sahib,' he said, 'I think, if we can, we should get away from here ek dum. Those boys may think better of it now and run off altogether. But they may still think they can deal with us and somehow get away with it.

'Let me see if I can just only get rid of that gag,' Ghote said.

Feeling a little as if he was intruding on someone's deepest privacy, he took hold of the Dean by both shoulders and turned him round. Then he set to work on the knot of the gag. It had been pulled together much more viciously than the rope, and for a while he thought he would have to leave the whole tie in place until they had got themselves to somewhere really safe. But at the last moment the tight twists of the knot began to give, and in a few seconds more the striped tie was clear of the Dean's mouth. He tossed it away.

'Well, Inspector,' came the familiar precise voice, 'you seem to have taken a dislike to that tie of mine. A pity. It is one of my favourites.'

Ghote actually turned away, stooped, retrieved the chewed and twisted piece of material and handed it back. He cursed himself as he did so, but he did it.

Then he looked round to see where they were. They seemed to be in a narrow dusty lane running along the backs of all the buildings opposite the college. Beside them lay a deep ditch, dry but for a few pools of black stagnant water, with a rusted fence of barbed wire on its far side.

But there should be access somewhere, he thought, back to the main road itself. Then in a few minutes they could be safe inside the college, and with the Dean seemingly no worse for all that had happened to him.

'Dean sahib,' he said, 'kindly come with after me. You feel able to walk?'

'Yes, Inspector. I have two legs. I can achieve locomotion.'

He made no answer. But he felt that the relationship between them was once again in full force, as galling as ever. Nor had he received a word of thanks for what he had done. What sort of a man was the fellow? And had he himself got to go back now to his role of stupid policeman? Well, perhaps that would be best after all. There might still be things to be learnt from this podgy intellectual, and, damn it, he was still far away from having an answer to report to the Centre.

He could not bring himself to look at the man he had rescued, the icy swine, other than in the most sideways manner as they both made their way along the rubbish-strewn dusty lane. But he was able to see that with every step he was walking more easily. There should be nothing wrong with him that a little massage and a cup of tea would not put right.

Before long they came to a gap between two of the buildings beside them, and Ghote led the way through.

It was not without a feeling of fizzy pleasure that he saw the big white slab of Oceanic College only some three hundred yards away.

Then, even more encouraging, ahead of them a tall figure came staggering out of the Paris Hotel and headed, limping badly but with evident determination, towards the tall gates of the college. Amar Nath. So those rich young goonda types had not succeeded in doing him any permanent damage.

And perhaps the bruises and wrenches he had received would teach him in future not to go rushing in when he had been told to be cautious.

Or perhaps not.

However, the fellow had done his share, as it had turned out, to rescue the Dean. So let him have credit.

'Dean sahib,' he said, remembering to produce to the full his bonehead police officer mode of speech, 'are you seeing who is along there? It is Amar Nath, college security officer. You are very much in his debt for becoming a free man once more. He was fighting those fellows like a tiger only.'

But all the Dean said in reply was 'Yes, Inspector, I do know the college has a security officer.'

Ghote did not explode at once. For a few moments he let the remark float in his mind like a single rich spongy gulab jamun all on its own in a wide bowl of syrup. So this was the sole response the man was going to make to being told, however lumpenly, that wretched rash Amar Nath had risked limb and perhaps life to rescue him. Not one single word of gratitude, any more than he had had himself. Only that contemptuous sneering. At a police officer who, however stupid he might seem, was there to protect such people as this fellow.

And then it came, a sudden unstoppable burning lava flow of sheer rage, spewing upwards.

He put out a hand, seized the Dean by the elbow and tugged him round.

'Now,' he barked. 'You listen to me for once in your damn conceited life.'

22

Ghote, despite a grating undertow that told him he was being more than foolish to alienate his best source of inside information, felt a rush of fierce delight at what he was doing to this supercilious, intolerable Dr Watson.

'Yes,' he repeated, letting the words rip out, 'you damn well listen to me. I have had altogether enough of your superiorities. Do you think you got out of that mess you were in by your own unaided powers? No, you are owing that to that altogether decent fellow Amar Nath. And to me also. And do you think I was coming to the rescue out of stupidity only? Not at all. I was weighing odds and deciding if your heart condition was so bad this was one and only thing to do. I tell you, Mr Dean, a Bombay Crime Branch officer is every bit as good at dealing with life problems as any damn academic. We are knowing what is going on in world. A hundred percent better than you ivory-tower wallas. And we are able to act on what we know. Which is worth one great deal more than sitting idle and telling other people to go and do whatsoever is coming into your head. So let me be hearing no more clever remarks from you. Now, or for ever.'

There it was done. It was out.

Now for the whiplash back.

But, to his amazement, all Dean Potdar said in answer, with only a trace of his customary waspishness, was 'Well, Inspector, if you choose to take that attitude, we had better part.'

And the fat little man went off, hobbling a little still, in the direction of the college.

Ghote stood where he was looking at him.

He felt a spreading area of surprise. He did not know exactly what he had expected in reply, but he had been fully prepared to get as good as he had given. More and worse even. And he had received nothing more than that almost mild parting shot.

So perhaps all was for the best. One burden was lifted from his shoulders, even though on the other hand he would no longer be able to consult this guru about the goings-on in the college.

That, however, might still prove a considerable disadvantage. After all, he still had no answer to the mystery Delhi so urgently wanted dealt with. He could not at this moment add one single word to the report he had begun cheerfully outlining as he had stepped out of Principal Bembalkar's chamber having discovered his keys had been left in his door.

He was equally far, too, from knowing the answer to what, to his mind at least, was the far more important thing, the mystery of who had added crushed tablets of Somnomax Five to the shrikhand that had been put in the way of that poor harijan dupe, Bala Chambhar.

Yes, it looked now as if Professor Kapur, spied at the time of the question-paper theft trying to break into the Student Union office, could not be responsible for the near-murder since he could not have been in possession of the stolen paper. And, again, it was hard to imagine someone as feeble as Victor Furtado had shown himself to be in the exam hall riot as ruthless enough to attempt murder, even on a sudden impulse.

Which left only Mrs Gulabchand.

Yet could he, simply on the grounds of that elimination, state in his report that the head of Oceanic College's English department had stolen the question-paper? No, he could not.

But what he could do, perhaps all the better for not being urged on by Dean Potdar, was to question Mrs Gulabchand again. To question her hard. If, when she had gone to her appointment with Principal Bembalkar to discuss this poet Hardy Thomas, she had actually entered his chamber despite her calm denial, then under pressure he might still catch her out in some small, significant discrepancy. The truth was, he thought, up to now he had let himself be overawed by the lady. It had been the effect, perhaps, of that atmosphere of academic superiority Dean Potdar had succeeded in imposing.

Well, he had blown that sky-high now.

So would he be able to manage better with Mrs Gulabchand? At least he would damn well see.

He glanced along the road. Both Amar Nath and Dean Potdar had vanished into the college. At a vigorous pace, despite the heat of the sun now near its peak, he set off in their wake.

No doubt Mrs Gulabchand would be lecturing to some class now that he wanted her. Just what he would expect in this damn business. And, after, he would be told that, although she ought to be taking another class, she had gone out of the building.

But he would wait. He would wait till midnight if he had to. And somewhere, either in the college or back in her flat, he would get hold of her and question and question her until he broke through.

When, however, he went to Mrs Cooper and asked where he could find the Head of the English Department she had only to consult an enormous timetable for a minute to say Mrs Gulabchand would have just finished one lecture and was not due to give her next for another hour. He would almost certainly find her in the staff common-room.

And he did. She came to the door herself in answer to his knock. More, he could see she was there alone. Nothing to stop him asking his questions, and going on asking them until he got answers that satisfied him.

'Madam,' he said, 'I was not altogether happy with what you were telling when we were last meeting.'

Standing in the doorway, he took a good look at the room in front of him.

Where would it be best to conduct this interrogation? He must not let Mrs Gulabchand, embodiment of Queen-Empress Victoria, place herself on any sort of throne. He himself was going to be the one occupying a dominating position.

Happily there seemed to be hardly anywhere in the dark, shabby-looking room, its walls lined with battered wooden lockers, to suit a queen-empress. The greater part of its space was filled by a wide table, left dusty in a long patch in its centre and dotted here and there with small piles of dingy books abandoned no doubt by other lecturers. Only at the head of this table, where there was a tall wooden chair somewhat more imposing than those pushed in at intervals along its length, was there anywhere Mrs Gulabchand might claim.

He walked boldly in, almost brushing the imposing figure who had opened the door, and claimed that head-of-the-table place.

'Madam,' he said, 'kindly sit.'

Mrs Gulabchand gave him a look of serene placidity.

'Yes, Inspector,' she said, 'I will sit. It is polite of you to ask me.'

But he was not going to be intimidated by this. He waited until Mrs Gulabchand had taken the chair on his right.

Then he leant forward.

'Madam,' he said, 'when I was asking your whereabouts at the time that question-paper was taken from Principal Bembalkar's chamber you were telling that you had gone just only into the outer office there and no more. Was that so?'

'Inspector, are you doubting my word?'

The rebuttal was put in the quietest of tones. But it was as firm as a wall of stone.

To Ghote, however, it was like the unexpected offer of a drink of cold water after being long out in the sun. Why had this Queen Victoria answered in that way when she could have simply replied that, yes, what she had told him before was so? Why instead had she challenged him? It must be to deflect any further pointed questioning.

But, if that was her object, she had misjudged her opponent.

'Mrs Gulabchand,' he said, not allowing the least trace of deference into his voice. 'To doubt itself is the duty of an investigating officer. I repeat: did you do no more than go into that outer office, see those keys in the Principal's door and leave?'

For several moments now Mrs Gulabchand sat in silence.

Why, Ghote thought. Why? If she really did just only what she told me before, why is she not saying so?

'Madam,' he interjected with sharpness, 'it is no good to pretend with me. You did not just only look at those keys, isn't it? Madam, you were entering the Principal's chamber.'

'Inspector,' Mrs Gulabchand said, without apparently losing any of the placidity she had retained ever since he had entered the room, 'let me explain.'

Then, at once, Ghote knew he was not going to hear that final answer. This calm woman, quietly agreeing she had told him a serious falsehood was no would-be murderer breaking down in face of unyielding questioning.

Inwardly he resigned himself.

'Very well,' he said. 'Kindly do explain.'

'Inspector, I went to see Principal Bembalkar that morning. We had, as I think you know, a long-arranged appointment. It was to discuss introducing the poetry of the novelist Thomas Hardy into our course, something I had felt was long overdue. So you can imagine I was surprised to find in the absence of the Principal's secretary his keys hanging in his door. I knew, as did everybody else in the college, that question-papers for the examinations had been delivered for safe-keeping to the Principal himself. We hear so much of cheating these days the arrangements to prevent it are endlessly discussed.'

'Yes, yes,' Ghote put in, beginning to be a little irked by the continuing calmness of her recital.

Mrs Gulabchand gave a sigh.

Ghote thought he detected in it a trace of shame. Was he after all mistaken then? Was the thief and the would-be murderer about to admit her crime after all?

'Inspector, I then did something which I have since regretted. Bitterly regretted.'

'Yes, madam?'

Suspense, tense as lightning-jittery clouds, tingled suddenly in his brain.

'Inspector, I decided that Principal Bembalkar should be taught a lesson. How I came to think that, why I came to think it, I shall never understand. I am not one for thoughtlessly laying down the law. I make my judgments, certainly. But I am no Dean – Well, let us say I hesitate to impose my views on others. But on this occasion, perhaps because I had allowed myself to be irritated by Dr Bembalkar's lack of politeness in forgetting our appointment, I decided, as I say, that he should be taught a lesson.'

Now. Now, despite everything, it was going to come, surely. She had gone in, she had seen the Statistical Techniques question-papers, she had taken the topmost copy, she had contrived to put it in Bala Chambhar's way. And then she had tried to cover up her action by getting rid of the young harijan. Yes, that must be it.

'Go on, madam,' he said, barely daring to speak.

'I saw that, although most of the newly-arrived question-papers had been put away, there on Dr Bembalkar's table – he must have been arranging them or something of the sort – was a pile of papers for the exam in Statistical Techniques.'

'And you took one?' Ghote could not now prevent himself asking directly. 'You took just only one?'

'No, Inspector. Certainly not. Or, that is, I did indeed reach out with the intention of taking away the whole pile. I admit to that, to my shame. But, as I did so, second thoughts prevailed. Why am I doing this, I thought. I turned and left the chamber.'

Ghote felt a deep grey sanddrift of disappointment swirling down towards him. He tried to fend it off. No, he told himself, this cannot be what happened. But he knew that it was. Why else would Mrs Gulabchand have admitted to him that she had entered the Principal's chamber? If she had in fact taken that single question-paper and had meant not to confess to it, she would have continued to deny and deny she had ever been in the room. But she had not denied it. She had told him plainly just what she had done.

Even to the point – he knew it for truth now – of saying she had withdrawn her hand as she had actually reached out to the pile of question-papers.

So now, not only was Professor Kapur apparently impossible as the thief, and Victor Furtado plainly too weak to have accomplished all the thief and near-murderer had done, but Mrs Gulabchand, the last suspect he had, was also to be struck from his list.

He got to his feet.

'Madam,' he said to the stout, sari-wrapped figure at the table beside him, 'I fully accept this explanation you have offered.'

He left her sitting, calm as ever, where she was and went out.

What to do, he asked himself. What to do?

How much time had passed, and here he was further away than ever from filling that gap between when the question-paper had been taken and when Bala Chambhar had begun to sell it. It could not be long before he got a message summoning him to the Additional Commissioner to explain. And he had no explanation to give.

Dean Potdar. He found himself longing to be able to go to the fat little malicious man once again to ask him to search his brain for any other possible new suspect, however unlikely. Was there perhaps after all some other ambitious person in the college who, at a pinch, might be a candidate for the Principal's seat? Or was there some other reason, however curious, why someone else might want to get rid of the Principal?

But he had burnt his boats with the Dean. That was certain.

He stood where he was, in the corridor a few yards along from the staff common-room, racking his brains. But when there came the sudden thunder and chatter of students released from their hour of classes, he had still not been able to conjure up the least semblance of a new suspect.

'There he is. There.'

The shout, though loud and close to, hardly penetrated his deep interior speculation. But what only a moment later did jerk him back to reality was the sight of an anger-contorted face, a face he seemed half to recognise, thrust close to his own.

'What – What – ' he jabbed out. 'What are you doing only?'

And as he shot out his startled question he realised whose face, just six inches from his own, he was looking at. The boy Amar Nath had knocked to the ground at the Paris Hotel.

Then, taking in at last things around him, he saw that, the boy confronting him was not alone. By no means. Beside him, in a grinning, ominous half-circle were, as far as he could make out, all the rest of Dean Potdar's kidnappers as well as a whole pressing cluster of other boys.

Were those rich riff-raffs now bent on revenge? Had he, lost in thought, allowed himself to be caught in a trap he would be lucky to get out of without some broken bones?

'What – What is this?' he asked, feeling not so much fright as bewilderment.

It was Mohinder Singh Mann, pushing towards him through the crowd, who answered.

'Inspector, you are being gheraoed.'

A gherao. Being surrounded by a crowd of protestors until they were granted their wish, whatever it was. Prevented from going anywhere, from taking a cold drink in the heat of the day, from having anything to eat, from visiting the mutri to relieve oneself even. Yes, but why were these students – the gherao was a typical student action – doing this? To him?

'But why?' he burst out. 'Why?'

Mohinder eased himself just into the front rank of the human wall.

'Inspector, it was not at all my idea.'

'No? Then what for are you here? What is this all?'

'Inspector, Sarita was making me come. She said we owed you that much. Inspector, these fellows are objecting to you interfering between them and the Dean. They want you out. Out of the college. It is not just only those friends of Shantaram Antrolikar. They have full backing. Only Sarita and myself – '

And then half a dozen hands grabbed the tall young Sikh and tugged him away.

Ghote, pressed hard up against the wall at his back, felt a dart of sadness. Why was it that this boy, so intelligent, so full of goodwill, so determined on justice, why was it that he and Sarita Karatkar, that spring-fresh hope who went with him, got pushed aside by crude, hectoring, thoughtless idiots like these hotheads? But that was the way of things.

Or perhaps it was not. Perhaps in the end, somehow, the Mohinder Singh Manns and Sarita Karatkars would triumph. They should. They had the force and the willingness to do it.

But, now, now what a bloody mess it was. What a bloody twisting and twining adage he had got himself yet more deeply into. How was he ever going to get out of it? How was he going to get himself disentangled?

He looked at the faces encircling him. Contorted with worked-up rage. Eyes bright with the pleasure of inflicting punishment. Taunting. Enjoying.

How was this possibly going to end?

23

All thought blotted out by sheer rage, Ghote looked at that ring of hostile, hate-filled, shouting, sneering and yelling faces.

Was there anyone likely to come to his rescue? He imagined Principal Bembalkar, sicklied o'er with the pale cast of thought, standing at the very far end of the corridor and bleating, as he had done when Bala Chambhar and his friends had blackened Victor Furtado's face, 'Gentlemen, as your senior I beg you . . .' He thought of Mrs Gulabchand, sitting in the staff common-room, no doubt placidly ignoring the noise only a few yards away. What had she said about that business with Furtado which equally she had heard taking place? Just something like 'There was some sort of jape'? No, quietly and unswervingly pursuing her own course, she would leave him to the mercy of his tormentors. Professor Kapur? Yes, he had acted with decision to quell the riot in the exam. But he would simply say now, without a doubt, that it was written in the stars one Inspector Ghote should be gheraoed for hours and hours on this day at this precise time. Amar Nath? Yes, he would come flying to the rescue. Only, he was almost certainly away somewhere nursing his bruises from his encounter with the ringleaders here.

So should he give in? Announce that he would leave? No, he could not. He would not. Damn it, he was a police officer on duty. He had been ordered to carry out an investigation in this bloody damn college. He could not just go away because a bunch of hot-headed students had decided he was interfering with some damn God-given right they had.

The right to kidnap their own Dean.

And that was somebody else who was not ever going to come to his rescue. However much, as the man responsible for college discipline, it was his bounden duty. But when it had been made clear to him that someone he had taken to be no more than a stupid police officer was not such, he had gone off, tail between his legs. He would delight now in not sending these riff-raffs about their business.

What a nasty little ungrateful malice-filled monkey he had turned out to be, acting always behind everybody's back.

Then, despite the noise and even heat coming in sickening waves from the ring of mocking students, into Ghote's head a slow dawning of light began to spread.

Dean Potdar. The fellow was just only a malice-filled monkey. Inside that black academic gown and that British-style intellectual's tweed jacket – in all this heat – he was no more than a nasty little mischief-maker. And . . . And surely that theft from Principal Bembalkar's chamber been first and foremost an act of mischief?

That was – yes, it must be – the missing motive he had not been able to think of even just a few seconds ago. Simple mischief. The monkey desire to play a trick.

No wonder he had been so blind since he had allowed himself to be guided and directed by the very man who had had the best opportunity of any of committing that theft. No wonder he had been unable to see the reason for the theft for what it was. How idiotic he had been. How truly stupid. Not how mock-stupid, how absolutely stupid.

Point after point came clicking into place as the menacing circle of angered faces so close to his own seemed to recede into an unimagined distance.

Yes, Dean Potdar with his office only a few yards away from the Principal's was, of course, in the best position to go in there when it had by chance been left unguarded. And, by God, the fellow must have just come back to his office from the common-room where he had seen the Principal arrive for his early lunch. Mrs Gulabchand had seen him there and had asked if he knew why Dr Bembalkar was not in his seat to keep his appointment with her.

And, now that he had begun to see the Dean in this light, he realised he had even had a first clue to it all almost as soon as he had come to the college, on the day after that torchlight morcha. Amar Nath had given it to him while they had been drinking horrible stewed tea in the Paris Hotel. Amar Nath had said then something about the Dean 'making nasty remarks' directed at everyone 'from Princi down'. So from then on he had had evidence himself that Dean Potdar despised and disliked Principal Bembalkar. And he had thought only at that time that this meant the Dean wanted the principalship.

Then, when he had foolishly, if understandably in the circumstances, sought the Dean's advice, since he was provenly out of the running as a contender for the principalship, the fellow had had the cunning to ask him what he knew about Bala Chambhar's chances of surviving what everybody then had believed to be attempted suicide. Of course, he would have been desperate to know whether his victim was safely out of the way, whether the poison he had put into that tub from a Monginis cake shop had worked. A Monginis, the sort of place someone as well-off as a college dean might well buy from. And, yes, at the corner of the Ramaprakash Housing Society block where the fellow was accustomed to go visiting his friends, the Gulabchands, there was a Monginis. He had seen the place with his own eyes.

In front of him the close-pressing circle of bodies swayed to and fro in excitement. He could smell a dozen different breaths, sharp with the odour of chewed paans, or still onion-reeking from the morning meal, or clinging with cigarette odour. Or merely foul.

But at the thought of how he had invaded the Gulabchands' flat side by side with the Dean a cold chill came over him. How he had allowed the fellow to dupe him. Because during the time they had been there – he was sure of this now – the Dean had contrived to send him to search the bathroom while slipping rapidly into the bedroom and planting in the nearer of the two bedside tables there the very packet of Somnomax Five he himself must have used. The Somnomax Five he must have bought to end those sleepless nights his secretary had jabbered out about when the fellow had been kidnapped.

Why had he not listened then instead of rushing to the fellow's rescue?

He knew too, he realised now, just when the transfer of the question-paper from actual thief to innocent, duped distributor had taken place. The Dean had had the infernal impudence to mention it to him, unless he had let it slip before he had had time to think. It had been when Bala Chambhar had been summoned to appear before him on a discipline charge 'just a few days ago', as he had said. It would have been the easiest thing in the world then to leave the room for a moment with that secret question-paper laid temptingly out for anti-social, indigent Bala to take, as later he must have managed to put the poisoned shrikhand in the boy's way.

And then what the fellow had done to him while all the time he had believed he himself was milking him for information. Purposefully and maliciously he had put suspect after suspect in his way, doing his best to send him into a state of utter confusion. And succeeding, damn it.

There had been Professor Kapur. And, yes, the astrologer had actually mentioned at his flat that he had heard of him from the Dean. That must have been only shortly before his visit, though it had not been clear at the time. And when Potdar had been there he must have seized the opportunity of putting that piece of Somnomax Five foil into the book on the table in the hall.

Then there was the way the fellow had added Victor Furtado to the list of suspects. Yes, of course, when just outside the hostel he had surprisingly encountered him, the fellow must have actually been on his way to plant Somnomax Five on the Goan. Damn it, he had had the cheek to try to send him off there in the wrong direction while he went round to do that. It had been only because he had happened to see Furtado giving his lecture to solitary Miss Washikar that he had got there before him. If his search of that bare room had taken place a little later, he would have come upon that seemingly damning evidence in place of the squashed box of stuff for countering foul interior gases. And the fellow had even made some attempt to include rakshas Mrs Cooper as a suspect.

What a fool to have run about here and there like that at that damn man's sweet will and pleasure.

Now the surrounding crowd of hostile young faces was less noisy. But no less determined.

No, Ghote thought, they have gheraoed people often before. They know how it is done. This is the start only of the long agony. They are saying to themselves there may be hours more before this fellow is breaking, but he will break before we do.

And would he?

Would the time come, with no rescue in sight, when the heat, thirst, perhaps hunger, or even the humiliation of needing to relieve himself, would force him into surrender?

But, damn it, that time was not yet. If they wanted a long, long battle of wills, then, by God, they would get same.

Deliberately he withdrew his thoughts and went back to enumerating all the points against the Dean he could think of. What a nasty, cunning creature the fellow was. That Day of Mourning device had been typical. He should have been alerted when he had learnt of it. From the pleasure the fellow so clearly had got in telling him what he had done, if from nothing else. It was a trick altogether typical of the man. Just like his attempting to make poor Principal Bembalkar look a fool. Just like his covering up that impulsive move by trying to poison Bala Chambhar and, typically again, not quite daring to use enough Somnomax Five to attain his object.

Suddenly he found floating in his head a curious expression. 'Letting I dare not wait upon I would.' Where had that come from?

Then he knew.

Back to his mind came that elusive page from his schooldays notebook. And now he saw the complete entry, in his round immature writing in English script. *Adage = a saying or maxim.*

So, damn it, he had not been caught up in any trap, or adage, after all. He was not the poor cat. He was not.

But he was still a man in deep trouble.

The ring of faces round him had sunk back into silent enmity now. But enmity it was. There and intent on staying there.

Then, in a flash of inspiration, he saw that he had a way out. A simple and almost foolproof way.

Without for an instant letting 'I dare not' wait upon 'I would', he addressed the silent faces.

'Listen, it is not myself you should be gheraoing. I am not the man who was announcing that Day of Mourning and taking away your Founder's Day holiday.'

'You were aiding and helping,' the boy Amar Nath had knocked down sullenly replied after a silent moment.

'All right, I was,' Ghote went on. 'But I am telling you now. I am not helping Dean Potdar any more. In fact, I am wanting just only one thing. To arrest the fellow on one serious charge.'

His words certainly caused a sensation in the close-clustered faces round him. He saw quick looks exchanged. Then, in a moment more expressions of incredulity.

Would it work? Would this stroke, thought up on the spur of the moment, make this mob change its mind? Had he bounced them into it?

He had. As suddenly as the mob had descended on him it parted.

'To Old Pot-belly,' someone shouted.

And in a moment the call was taken up, it seemed, by every boy in the mob.

'To Old Pot-belly. To Old Pot-belly.'

The tone, too, had changed completely. Where, when he had first been surrounded, every face was angry, now a sudden spirit of laughter ran everywhere.

'To Old Pot-belly. Arrest Old Pot-belly. Prison for Pot-pot. Prison for Pot-pot.'

Ghote furiously wished he had not gone as far as he had. He was being swept along now by these noisy brainless devils in a wild rush to the Dean's office. Were they expecting him to arrest the fellow there and then? Well, he had more or less said that that was what he intended to do. But he could have said nothing less if he had wanted to break up the gherao.

Now he was at the top of the stairs. He was round on to the offices veranda. He was outside the Dean's door. He was inside the outer office. The Dean's secretary had risen to her feet. Once more her knitting had fallen to the ground leaving a long trail of pink wool from the needles she still grasped.

'Arrest Old Pot-belly. Arrest. Arrest. Arrest.'

The shouts had grown in volume till they had become a roar.

And then the inner door opened and Dean Potdar stood there.

'What – What – Go away,' he said, his voice getting feebler with every word.

And now the yelling students round Ghote had fallen back a little and every face was looking at him. With avid expectation.

But he could not effect an arrest just like that. These things had to be done in the proper way. There had to be two panches there to witness what the accused had said. He ought to have obtained the Additional Commissioner's backing.

'Inspector Ghote ki jai,' one of the mob shouted now.

Victory to Inspector Ghote. Was that what they wanted? Were insisting on?

Then abruptly Dean Potdar himself came to his rescue.

'Arrest me?' he said, stepping half a pace forward and glaring at Ghote. 'And just why do you think you can do that, Inspector?'

Now, Ghote thought. Now I can get him. He has laid himself open to interrogation. And, after all, I do have witnesses. Twenty–thirty of them.

'Mr Potdar,' he said, 'I have reason to believe that you were offering to one Bala Chambhar, student at this college, a quantity of shrikhand into which you had put a certain poison.'

'Somnomax Five,' the Dean shot back, with a look of piggy triumph. 'And how are you going to prove I ever had any of that?'

Then Ghote smiled.

'It is altogether simple,' he said. 'I have told no one whatsoever until now that I had reason to believe the substance used to attempt the murder of Bala Chambhar was Somnomax Five. But you are knowing it. Mr Potdar, I am arresting you on a charge of attempted murder.'

24

It was only when Ghote was seated at his desk at Headquarters, with Dean Potdar safely lodged in a cell, that he began to have a new attack of doubts about what he had so impulsively done.

Had he really got enough evidence to take to court? He had no proof of any link between Bala Chambhar and the Dean, beyond the Dean's remark that he had had the boy up before him on a disciplinary matter. True, he could probably obtain some sort of evidence that at least that had happened. But he would never be able to get evidence that at that interview the stolen question-paper had been put where Bala was likely to see it and steal it in his turn. Nor had he a scrap of evidence that the Dean had entered Principal Bembalkar's chamber. True, he might be able to get the Dean's secretary to remember that he had left his office during the time the question-paper had been taken. But that was far from being proof that he had taken it. Again, he might find some gumasta at that branch of Monginis who might recognise the Dean and recall that he had bought shrikhand at about the time he must have done. And perhaps he could find where the Dean had obtained his supply of Somnomax Five, unless that had been smuggled goods as it well might have been. No, the chain of proof had appalling gaps in it.

Despite catching Potdar out with that admission that he knew Somnomax Five was the poison used on Bala Chambhar, he was still far from being sure of eventually obtaining a conviction. What he needed was for Bala never to have impulsively eaten that tub of shrikhand. Without the boy's evidence of having seen the stolen question-paper in the Dean's office he was never going to have a case that was other than damn leaky at every joint.

Yet he was as certain as could be that the Dean, not letting 'I dare not' wait upon 'I would', had snatched up that paper from Principal Bembalkar's desk when with his monkey curiosity he had gone poking and prying into the chamber that should have been locked. No doubt about it, he had seen an opportunity of gravely wounding the man he disliked so much and, without weighing the consequences, he had acted. And, once he had passed that paper on to Bala, he had again suddenly realised what he had laid himself open to. Then, without much thought, he had simply bought a sweet treat he knew the boy would like, crushed up some of his sleeping tablets into it and had put it in the boy's way.

That was what had happened. A series of spur-of-the-moment actions. They had happened. But without Bala there was no proof of any of the vital links in the chain.

Damn it, damn it, damn –

His telephone rang. It was the Additional Commissioner.

Slowly he pushed himself to his feet. He would have one hell of a lot of explaining to do, and he very much doubted if any of his explanations would be accepted.

But at least he now had a good account of what had happened to the Statistical Techniques question-paper, and the Centre, while it would be no doubt delighted to learn there was no possibility of any political fall-out, would not want the sort of proof of his account a court of law would require.

He snatched up his report, which he had typed with extraordinary care. And, he said to himself, this is a hell of a lot fatter, and better thought-out, than that single sheet the CBI wallas produced. There was that. Perhaps it would be enough to check the Additional Commissioner's wrath.

But he went up the spiral staircase to the great man's cabin with leaden steps.

'Sir,' he said the very moment he had clicked heels in front of the huge sweep of a desk. 'Sir, I beg to hand over my report on one missing question-paper, Statistical Techniques.'

The Additional Commissioner looked up at him with a faint air of surprise.

'Ah, that,' he said. 'Did no one tell you, Ghote, that the Centre no longer requires any report?'

'Sir, no. Sir, but why? Why?'

'Inspector, it is not for you – it is not for any of us – to question the decisions of the Centre. I dare say they had their reasons. Let us leave it at that. And, now, Ghote, what is this business of the arrest of the Dean of that college out there, whatever it's called?'

'Oceanic College, sir.'

'Yes, yes. Oceanic College. But what I want to know is why was that fellow arrested and charged without a word to myself? I am not here, Ghote, just to play games with pieces of paper. I am here to – '

The ringing of his telephone had interrupted him.

'Haan? Haan? What is it?'

The great man listened.

'But why are you telling me this, Doctor?' he said after a few seconds. 'Do you know who you're speaking to? I am the Additional Commissioner, Crime Branch. I hardly think you can want me.'

A jabber of disclaimer at the far end.

'Ghote?' the Additional Commissioner snapped when it had come to an end. 'You want Inspector Ghote? Well, I suppose he's here, so you had better get on with it. But be damn quick about it.'

He thrust the receiver across to Ghote.

'It is Inspector Ghote?'

'Yes, yes. Who is that?'

'Dr Shah here, Inspector. KEM Hospital.'

'Dr Shah? Oh, yes. Yes?'

What could this be?

'Inspector, I am thinking, since you were showing so much interest in that boy in Bed 52, you would be glad to know we have succeeded to deal with that poison. A technique I myself am inventing. Tip-top results.'

Ghote thought.

'You are saying Bala Chambhar will live, Doctor?'

'Yes, yes. Of course. My treatment. Already he is speaking a little. Just now only he was muttering some words. Not distinguishable, of course. Something like *Potdar shrikhand*. Something like that. But significant. Altogether significant, medically speaking.'

Ghote put the receiver back and began happily explaining.

One more telephone call came through for Ghote before he left his cabin at the end of that day. It was from Principal Bembalkar.

Ghote was surprised.

'What it is I can do for you, sir?' he asked.

'Nothing, Inspector, nothing. I simply wanted to tell you my news. To tell somebody somehow sympathetic. And, besides Mrs Cooper who has gone to her child who is sick, I find there is no one.'

'Yes, sir?'

'Yes. You see, Inspector, I have made up my mind at last and resigned as Principal of Oceanic College. From now on I am going to devote myself entirely to *Hamlet*. I shall call my book – it is an interpretation of the play as a study of the vice of indecision – I shall call it *The Pale Cast of Thought*.'

'Sir, that is most interesting,' Ghote said.

It was all he could think of to say.

Then one more thing came into his mind.

'Sir, I am sure you are altogether happy to have put aside those responsibilities you were having. Sir, congratulations. And, sir, can you please be telling me: is it Professor Kapur who is to take your seat? He was saying once such is written in his stars.'

'No, no, Inspector. I do not think Kapur was ever really considered. Mrs Rajwani thinks he is too – but, never mind that. No, this is just between us for the time being, you understand.'

'Yes, sir.'

'Well then, it seems Mrs Rajwani has recently made the acquaintance of one of the college staff she had not hitherto met, and she seems to think he will suit her – That is, she believes he is eminently suitable for the post.'

'Oh, yes, sir? It is . . . ?'

'A fellow called Furtado, Inspector. Victor Furtado. I don't know if you met him.'

So at last Inspector Ghote made his way home, still revolving in his mind all that had happened to him since the time he had been called to the Additional Commissioner's office to learn that a question-paper in Statistical Techniques had been sold in the streets of Bombay in advance of the day when the examination was to be held.

But it was not until he was standing outside his own door that it occurred to him that this, once more, would be an evening when Ved would be busy with the affairs of the Regals cricket club.

An evening when he could accomplish what he had made up his mind he had to do just before that first summons to the Additional Commissioner had come. To beat his wife.

He stood there for a moment, for several long moments, thinking.

Then he tapped at the latch.

Protima was quick to open to him.

'For once,' she said, 'you are in good time. But how hot you are looking. Come inside, come inside. Sit. I will fetch you a cold Mangola. I know that is what you are most liking.'

'No,' Ghote said. 'No, I am always preferring Limca. Please get me that.'

Protima dipped her head in assent, little Hindu wife.

'In one moment only,' she said.

Ghote stepped in and kicked off his shoes.

Yes, he thought to himself, it is as I was thinking just now before coming in. That is the way a man and his wife should be. There is no need for all those hasty measures, all that beating and so forth some fellows are boasting about. But neither is there any need for shilly-shally. It is just only a question of stating calmly what you are wanting, and you would get same. To one hundred percent.

And besides, he added to himself, if you are listening to your wife in a reasonable way, then you would accept it when she is offering one sensible suggestion. Like, for example, that there could be some other reason than wanting to succeed to a college principalship for anyone to have taken a question-paper from the Principal's chamber.